ONLY MADNESS

(A Sadie Price FBI Suspense Thriller—Book 6)

Rylie Dark

Rylie Dark

Bestselling author Rylie Dark is author of the SADIE PRICE FBI SUSPENSE THRILLER series, comprising six books (and counting); the MIA NORTH FBI SUSPENSE THRILLER series, comprising six books (and counting); the CARLY SEE FBI SUSPENSE THRILLER, comprising six books (and counting); and the MORGAN STARK FBI SUSPENSE THRILLER, comprising three books (and counting).

An avid reader and lifelong fan of the mystery and thriller genres, Rylie loves to hear from you, so please feel free to visit www.ryliedark.com to learn more and stay in touch.

Copyright © 2022 by Rylie Dark. All rights reserved. Except as permitted under the U.S. Copyright Act of 1976, no part of this publication may be reproduced, distributed or transmitted in any form or by any means, or stored in a database or retrieval system, without the prior permission of the author. This ebook is licensed for your personal enjoyment only. This ebook may not be re-sold or given away to other people. If you would like to share this book with another person, please purchase an additional copy for each recipient. If you're reading this book and did not purchase it, or it was not purchased for your use only, then please return it and purchase your own copy. Thank you for respecting the hard work of this author. This is a work of fiction. Names, characters, businesses, organizations, places, events, and incidents either are the product of the author's imagination or are used fictionally. Any resemblance to actual persons, living or dead, is entirely coincidental. Jacket image Copyright oleshko andrey, used under license from Shutterstock.com.
ISBN: 978-1-0943-7964-7

BOOKS BY RYLIE DARK

SADIE PRICE FBI SUSPENSE THRILLER
ONLY MURDER (Book #1)
ONLY RAGE (Book #2)
ONLY HIS (Book #3)
ONLY ONCE (Book #4)
ONLY SPITE (Book #5)
ONLY MADNESS (Book #6)

MIA NORTH FBI SUSPENSE THRILLER
SEE HER RUN (Book #1)
SEE HER HIDE (Book #2)
SEE HER SCREAM (Book #3)
SEE HER VANISH (Book #4)
SEE HER GONE (Book #5)
SEE HER DEAD (Book #6)

CARLY SEE FBI SUSPENSE THRILLER
NO WAY OUT (Book #1)
NO WAY BACK (Book #2)
NO WAY HOME (Book #3)
NO WAY LEFT (Book #4)
NO WAY UP (Book #5)
NO WAY TO DIE (Book #6)

MORGAN STARK FBI SUSPENSE THRILLER
TOO LATE (Book #1)
TOO CLOSE (Book #2)
TOO FAR GONE (Book #3)

CHAPTER ONE

This was reckless, to say the least.

Maddie Heard had been having serious doubts about this decision. And, now that they were actually standing on the chilly blacktop, she had a really bad feeling. She shook her head as her younger sister, Lydia, waved at the oncoming truck, sticking out her thumb in the familiar gesture of a hitchhiker.

"Lydia, I don't think this is a good idea," she protested, her voice muffled through her scarf. Mid-February in Alaska wasn't a fun time to be out in the sticks like this. Trucker country, where there was nothing on either side of the long, deserted highway apart from the occasional rundown diner and restroom and miles and miles of snow on either side. The gray slush of the snow seemed to blend in with the horizon, bleeding into a gray, cloudy sky, and the seemingly endless sameness was giving Maddie a headache.

"So, what do you suggest we do?" Lydia asked, looked over her shoulder with disdain. "Walk? I'm not going back home. I've had enough of that filth." Grimacing in disgust, she held her sister's eyes. Maddie nodded.

Lydia was right. They couldn't go back, and they didn't have anywhere else to go. They couldn't afford the rent on their mother's place after she had died, and their only family had been an aunt and uncle. But they were tired of living with two people who argued all the time, and who both drank heavily. Their cramped little house was a mess, the kitchen was infested with roaches, and it was clear that Aunt Stella and Uncle Bob didn't care about Maddie and Lydia, or much else, at all.

They had a second cousin in Anchorage, who they hadn't seen for years, who might not even be at the same address, but it had to be worth a shot. Perhaps this cousin wouldn't mind putting them up for a few weeks while they got on their feet. And if not, a big city would be a better place to look for work and a cheap motel. But it meant catching a ride with a stranger, and right now, Maddie was wary of strangers.

Her fear of getting into an unknown vehicle flared up when the truck that Lydia had been flagging down stopped by the roadside. A window rolled down and a friendly-looking face peered out with a smile. Lydia looked back at her sister, excited, and Maddie stepped forward. The driver looked harmless, but how could you really tell? The one that had brought them this far had turned out to be a real creep.

But it was either that or stay freezing by the roadside. They had already walked for what felt like miles. And at this time of night there might not be another potential ride for hours.

"Where are you girls going?"

"Anchorage," Maddie said politely. The cab door swung open.

"I can take you part of the way at least. Get in."

Maddie hesitated, but Lydia was already clambering eagerly up into the seat. She was like a young deer, skinny and tall, but already a beauty, with classic, perfect features. Maddie, a year older, was the plain, sensible one, but she couldn't resent her sister.

Lydia was all she had, and she had sworn to protect her. Always.

Maddie climbed in after her and shut the door, feeling a shudder go through her as she did so. The feeling of being trapped. But Lydia was chatting away happily with the truck driver, who pulled off, seemingly anxious to get back on the road. Everything seemed fine, normal, but Maddie couldn't shake off a sense of foreboding.

Maybe she was just worried, now that she was on the road, about what awaited them in Anchorage. Finding their cousin was a slim hope, and she might not welcome them even if they did locate her. What if they ended up homeless, or worse? At nineteen, Maddie was responsible for Lydia, who was only a year younger but seemed a lot more childish. Maddie drummed her fingers on the window, watching the gray landscape whizz past. Lydia chattered on, and the truck driver seemed happy to listen to her.

They really were all the way out in the middle of nowhere, Maddie thought, wondering when the lights of Anchorage would come into view. Probably not for another few hours, she guessed.

At that moment, the truck slowed and they pulled over, the driver sighing heavily.

"One minute, girls. There's a hose fitting loose in the back. I can hear it starting to rattle. I need to stop and tighten it up."

"I'll help. I'd like some fresh air," Lydia offered, already scrambling over Maddie's lap to get out as the truck jolted to a stop.

"That'll be appreciated." The driver looked pleased.

"You stay here," Lydia told her sister. She had always minded the cold less than Maddie. The two of them climbed out, and Maddie watched them in the wing mirror. Lydia was talking animatedly as she disappeared from view, her hands waving. She was already happier after getting out of that house, Maddie thought. It had been the right thing. Whatever awaited them had to be better than what they had left. She would make sure of it.

Staring out of the window, she realized there wasn't a soul to be seen, even though the bleak horizon stretched for miles. It felt as if the three of them might be the only living people in this harsh, empty landscape. There wasn't even another set of headlights on this narrow, empty road, and hadn't been for a while.

She felt a thud come from the back of the truck. Was that the hose getting tightened, she wondered, with a feeling of sudden doubt. It had sounded heavier than a hose should.

Then silence followed. Silence that she thought stretched on for longer than it should. With a surge of worry, she wondered if something was wrong.

"Lydia?" Maddie called, chills prickling her spine. She tried to unclip her seatbelt to go and see what was going on, but it was jammed. As she wrestled with it, she saw movement out of the corner of her eye in the wing mirror and she looked up, hoping to see Lydia.

What she saw instead froze her blood in her veins.

The truck driver was moving swiftly towards her door, the smile gone, eyes glittering with menace. There was no sign of Lydia.

And suddenly, Maddie knew that she was never going to reach Anchorage.

CHAPTER TWO

This waiting felt like it would kill her.

FBI agent Sadie Price had been at Sheriff Cooper's place for an hour, after forensics had met them in the mine shaft to collect the bones they had found. A skeleton of a woman, over twenty years old, with scraps of fabric from a red dress still clinging to her.

And a totem around her neck that meant the skeleton could be Sadie's mother.

Now all she could do was wait for someone from the forensics lab to get back to her and tell her if she was right. So far it had been the longest hour of her life.

She sat on Cooper's couch, her hands grasping a mug of strong coffee, staring down at the wooden totem that she had removed from the skeleton's neck. The Inuit words engraved into it stared out at her, confirming her worst fears.

Mother Dawn. The name that the residents of the Inuit village had given to her mother, in honor of the midwifery services that she had performed for them. Her mother had been well-loved, even by Sadie's brute of a father.

So how had she ended up dead?

Sadie's mother had disappeared when she was seven, and Jessica, her older sister by two years, had become her main caregiver when their father's drinking had gotten out of hand. Sadie had adored Jessica, but then her sister had disappeared too when Sadie was fifteen, only for her body to be fished out of a frozen lake a few days later.

Sadie had been hunting for her sister's killer ever since, but the clue that she had expected to lead her to the answers – her father's map, drawn as he lay dying in the hospital – had led her to the skeleton in the mineshaft instead.

"I just don't know what to think about it all," she said without looking at Cooper. "Is this connected to Jessica's death, and what if the remains aren't my mother's? What does that mean?" She shook her head, feeling overwhelmed by it all. She was fresh from solving a horrific serial killer case in Anchorage and had barely managed a day's rest in between that and finding the skeleton.

She needed a vacation. But she also knew that she wouldn't be going anywhere until this was solved.

"Whatever it is," Cooper murmured, placing a hand on her back, and running it gently up and down, "we'll figure it out. You're not on your own."

Sadie had never been a particularly affectionate person and would have flinched away from partners trying to touch her like this in the past, but somehow, with Cooper, it was different. After an antagonistic start working together on another serial case last year, they had become firm friends and then, very recently, lovers.

And that was the right word. Although she wasn't ready to admit it out loud, maybe not even to herself, Sadie loved Logan Cooper with an intensity that scared and thrilled her by turns. She leaned into his touch, allowing herself a few minutes of comfort.

"What if I never find out?" It was perhaps her biggest fear. No matter what horrors she discovered, it would be worse never knowing what had happened to her family. Especially to Jessica. Sadie had felt like the walking wounded since her sister's death. No matter how many killers she caught or criminals she took down, she wouldn't be satisfied until she had caught whoever murdered her sister.

And now her mother, too?

"Forensics shouldn't take too long," Cooper reassured her. "Why don't you get some sleep? We were up before dawn to go the mine shaft. I need to go down to the station to relieve Jane, and she will come straight back and go to bed herself after a night shift. So, you won't be disturbed."

Sadie smiled, grateful for the offer, although she wondered what Jane, Cooper's sister and deputy, would say to find Sadie in her brother's bed for a second morning. Most likely, Sadie thought, she would be happy for them both. But she wasn't sure if she wanted their fledgling relationship to be local news just yet.

"Thank you. I'll phone Caz and let her know where I am." Caz was her proprietor and friend, and owner of the local saloon. A big, rough woman with a heart as soft as her outward exterior was hard, she was Sadie's best friend in Anchorage. She adored Caz's daughter, Jenny, too. She rented Caz's spare room, but it was small and cramped and, being next to the saloon, pretty damn noisy. She would get a much better sleep in Cooper's bed.

Sadie was about to take herself upstairs when her phone rang. She snatched at it, hoping wildly it would be the forensics team even though it was far too soon. Her heart sank when she saw that it was Paul Golightly, her ASAC at Anchorage FBI Field Office. He was her boss, and a good guy. If he was calling her this early in the morning, then there was something wrong.

Unless it was about the job. Golightly had offered her the position as Senior Agent, which was a step up and would make her career, but she had asked for time to think about it. Until she had solved the mystery of her sister's death and her mother's disappearance, she knew there was no way that she could make such big decisions about her future.

She had never planned on staying in Alaska, and had always assumed her time here would be temporary. She had come back to recuperate after a high-profile case that had nearly killed her, to finally confront her past demons and lay her sister to rest. She had never expected to build a life here. Never expected she would find enough to keep her here, but perhaps now, she saw, she'd been wrong.

"Special Agent Price," she answered, hoping against hope this was a social call, even though she knew it wouldn't be. Golightly was fond of her, but not that fond.

"Price," he said, as straight to the point as ever. "I want to know if you're ready to head up to Fairbanks."

"Fairbanks?" Sadie blinked in surprise. "I thought we agreed I was having a few days off after the Anchorage case."

"We did," Golightly conceded, "But you're the best agent I have, and I knew you'd want me to call you in an emergency. If you don't want to take this case, it's fine. But if you do, I'd appreciate it. A lot."

"What's happened?" From his tone, she knew this was bad.

"Two young women – only just adults, from the description I've been given - have been found dead in a restroom just outside Fairbanks. One of the trucker stops."

Sadie nodded, forgetting that Golightly couldn't see her. She knew the area he meant. The highway stretched for miles, across a desolate landscape between small towns. You could see no one between stops apart from the odd hitchhiker. It was a good place to disappear. And, it seemed, a good place to kill.

She swallowed. Young murder victims, and women especially, were particularly heartrending to deal with. No matter how many bodies she saw, she never forgot a single victim. But she had learned how to keep a neutral face and not throw up in the morgue.

"How were they killed?"

She heard Golightly suck in his breath.

"Head wounds. Deep, brutal, and look to have been instantly fatal." Sadie felt her stomach sink, but she stood up, already putting her hopes for a rest to one side.

"I'm leaving now. Send me the exact address."

"Keep me posted," Golightly said, and was gone.

Cooper had stood up behind her, his hands kneading her shoulders. She turned to him and put her arms around him without speaking, laying her head on his chest, and enjoying the warmth of him for just a moment before pulling away.

"I've got to go," she said with a sigh. "If you hear anything from forensics...?"

"I'll be in touch straight away," Cooper told her. He was gazing at her, but she couldn't look at him, suddenly afraid she might cry. Cooper had seen her in vulnerable positions before, but not *that* vulnerable. She had to hold on to at least some of her carefully constructed defenses.

Sadie left and got into her truck, putting everything else in the back of her mind and concentrating on the information that Golightly had given her. Two young women...she wondered if they were hitchhikers. There were always a few hanging around the truck stops, hoping to catch rides to a faraway destination, better place, a better future. Sometimes, they went missing, and although everyone always hoped they had just skipped town or moved to a state where there were better pickings, Sadie had no doubt many of them were as yet unknown murder cases.

But these victims hadn't disappeared, had they? Sadie wondered what she was about to find.

CHAPTER THREE

This was going to be bad. Sadie knew it as soon as she saw the look on the state trooper's face. It was a look Sadie had seen too many times in her career as a Behavioral Unit Analysis Special Agent, most usually on the faces of other federal agents. In Alaska though, she was as likely to be working with state troopers and county sheriffs as she was with other FBI agents.

"Agent Price? I'm Officer Cowell." The trooper looked to be about thirty, blonde and with the sort of good looks that were impossible not to notice. He didn't have the rugged handsomeness of Cooper, but rather a fresh-faced, model look as though he had stepped out of a boy band. Right now, though, his topaz eyes were clouded. Whatever Sadie was about to see at the rest stop, which was a lonely, cold, four-hour drive from Anchorage, it had horrified this trooper.

"Who found the victims?" Sadie asked, shaking his hand. Cowell grimaced.

"A woman on a cross-country ski trip. The group stopped for her to use the restrooms, and she walked straight into the stall where the bodies had been left." His breath curled visibly on the freezing air. She wondered how long he had been standing out here waiting for her, avoiding having to go back into that bathroom.

"They were left in one stall, both of them? Do we have an ID on the victims?"

Cowell hesitated before he replied. "Yeah. A rucksack was on the floor next to them, it had their ID and clothes and cash inside. The cash wasn't taken. I'm guessing they were hitchhiking; it's pretty common along this stretch. The bodies look like they've been moved and dumped."

For a second the full disgust and shock he was feeling was visible on Cowell's face and Sadie felt a wave of sympathy, guessing this was the first time the state trooper had seen a homicide like this.

"You didn't tell me their names," she pressed gently.

Although she would see for herself in just a few minutes, she was interested to get the officer's first, horrified, impressions. Killers who moved their victim's bodies were doing so for a reason – which was often either to hide them, or else to make them easier to find. This seemed like it was the second of the two scenarios.

"Sorry." Cowell ran a hand across his chin. "Madeline and Lydia Heard, from Tacoma. Madeline was nineteen and Lydia eighteen. Fairbanks PD are running them through the system now; they'll notify the family."

Sadie nodded, wondering how welcoming the Fairbanks police department was going to be to the involvement of both state troopers and the FBI. In her experience, the different agencies didn't always work well together and federal involvement was often resented. On her first case with Cooper, he had been less than happy with her presence. His sister Jane had been downright hostile.

But Sadie had little time for the internal politics of law enforcement. She wanted to know who had killed these girls, and why. The fact that they were sisters, and close in age, just like herself and Jessica, made her chest ache.

"Let's go in," Sadie said heavily, bracing herself for the scene. She followed Cowell into the rest stop and towards the women's bathroom, which was now cordoned off with police tape. Cowell stepped over it and held the bathroom door open for her, and she had to wonder if that was done out of politeness or because he didn't want to go in first.

Sadie entered the dingy bathroom, which smelled of floral air freshener and dampness. The door to the first stall was open, and Sadie had to stop herself from gasping out loud.

The two Heard sisters were lying at the back of the stall, their features splashed with blood from what looked to be one deep head wound inflicted on each victim. She wondered what the killer had used to do his deadly work. There was a lot of rage in these blows. The victims must have died instantly. *Crude*, she thought, *but quick*.

The bodies had clearly been moved after death, as she could see scuffs on the floor and a blood smear on the wall. They'd been shunted roughly side by side, and displayed face up. Sadie felt the ache in her chest again but kept her face carefully impassive, although she could already tell this case was going to be one that tugged at her emotions. Sometimes that could be a good thing, but Sadie also knew it could make any agent rash, too hasty in their response.

She took a deep breath as her eyes swept their bodies, wishing this was something she didn't have to see. They were fully clothed, and apart from the head wounds, she didn't see any immediate signs of a struggle. No obvious defensive injuries, although she knew the postmortem might pick up more information.

She took a deep breath, closing her eyes momentarily against the painful sight.

Some cases were more personal than others. And with the potential discovery of her mother's bones weighing over her, Sadie was finding it much harder than usual to keep her professional demeanor.

"It's horrible, isn't it?" Cowell said behind her, his voice catching slightly.

"Do we know if there were any witnesses?" Sadie asked. "Security camera footage, maybe?"

Cowell took a moment to answer, and Sadie deliberately avoided looking at him, letting him regain his composure. "The camera's broken. Other than the woman that found them, no one has come forward yet, but Fairbanks PD have sent an alert out. There will be a news item about it at lunchtime, calling for witnesses and giving a hotline number that members of the public can contact. It's doubtful; this stretch of road is pretty deserted, but we can hope."

Sadie nodded, thinking that at this time of year, with activity on the roads low, the killer might not have been seen at all. They'd need a lucky break to find out more, and would need to search carefully for any evidence that could point the way.

Something caught her eye on the younger girl's shoes, and she crouched down, careful not to get too close or disturb anything.

"Forensics are on their way," Cowell said, echoing her thoughts.

"There are scuff marks on the back of Lydia's sneakers," Sadie said, standing up. "Fresh dirt. It looks as though she's been dragged along the ground. Let's have a look around outside and see if we can see where from."

Cowell followed her out of the bathroom without speaking. Back outside in the frigid air, Sadie saw two police officers also emerging from the sitting area, with a group of four men and women dressed in skiing gear. Sadie walked over to introduce herself, noticing the grim looks on the faces of the two police officers, one male and one female, both of them looking a lot younger than Sadie's own twenty-nine years.

"Agent Price," the male officer said wearily, "thank you for coming. I'm Detective Johnson and this is Detective Lopez. You've seen the bodies? Do you need to question the witness who found them? I've taken a statement. She didn't touch anything, or even get close, and saw nobody else around."

Sadie looked at the group with sympathy, taking in their shocked faces.

"There's no need for that," she said. "If we have a statement from her, and she saw nothing suspicious, these folks can go."

"Thank you." The two detectives seemed to be grateful for her presence, which was refreshing, but she could well understand why they would be happy for her to take the lead on this, at least until they established what was happening here.

Sadie knew the importance of not jumping to conclusions, but it was hard to ignore a decade of working with serial killer cases as her main area of expertise. This killing screamed red flags at her, of a homicidal murderer who would not stop here.

"Have there been any other local cases like this?"

"No, thank goodness," Johnson said with a shudder. Lopez's eyes flew wide open.

"You think there could be more?"

"Routine question," Sadie said. There was no use in voicing what was, as yet an unfounded intuition. "I take it you guys are going to notify the victims' family?"

Johnson nodded. "We're just waiting for forensics."

"I'm going to have a look around," Sadie told them. "There were fresh marks on Lydia's shoes that look like she's been recently dragged on the ground. It could be nothing, but it's worth a look."

She left them standing outside the rest stop and followed along the roadside shoulder with Cowell silently in step next to her, scanning the ground ahead.

"There," he said, pointing to recent marks in the icy mud along the side of the road. Sadie felt her heart quicken as she hurried over and crouched down to inspect the marks. They looked, indeed, like fresh drag marks. The sort that might be made if you were dragging a body – or unconscious person – perhaps by pulling them under the arms, with their heels dragging in the dirt.

She stood back up and walked the length of the drag marks, noticing tire tracks near the end of them where a truck had clearly pulled up on the shoulder. The drag marks were about the length of a truck trailer, and Sadie knew she was looking at the spot where the killer had pulled up and taken his prey from the truck into the bathroom.

"Do you know anything about trucks?" Sadie asked Cowell as he came up alongside her, his eyes scanning the marks. He seemed quick on the ball, if a touch green around the ears, Sadie thought.

"My pop was a trucker," he said, bending down to get a good look at the tire marks.

"Do they tell you anything about the make and model of the truck or tires?" Sadie asked. It was probably too much to hope for, but an unusual tire tread or type of truck could make tracking the murderer down a lot easier. Otherwise, it could potentially be like a needle in a haystack. Dozens of truckers regularly used this route, and with the lack of camera footage and the isolation of the place, leads could be hard to come by, unless the crime scene itself yielded anything useful.

DNA would be great, she thought ruefully, but she rarely got that lucky.

"Looks like a common enough tread," Cowell said with a disappointed sigh as he straightened up, "but I could be wrong."

Sadie waved Johnson and Lopez over and showed them what they had found. "Forensics will take pictures and molds of the tracks," Johnson nodded, his eyes narrowing as he surveyed the scene, no doubt, as Sadie had, recreating what had happened here. "Maybe we'll get a lucky hit."

"Let's hope so," Sadie murmured. She walked away from the small group, taking deep breaths of the cold Alaskan air, and trying not to think of the two sisters behind her in the bathroom, robbed of their lives by a brutal killer.

Was he targeting young women in particular, she mused, or was it just the fact they were alone and vulnerable? It had to be a crime of opportunity, Sadie guessed, given the likelihood the girls were hitchhiking and had been picked up by a trucker, but it was too soon to rule out other possibilities. He could have been known to them, taking them somewhere. But she suspected the first scenario was the most plausible.

Where had they been going, she wondered, and perhaps more importantly, had they been running from something?

An approaching vehicle caught her eye, pulling her out of her thoughts. Forensics had arrived.

Time for some answers.

CHAPTER FOUR

A tire iron. That appeared to be what had killed the girls.

Sadie and Cowell stood opposite the medical examiner at Fairbanks morgue; the bodies laid out side by side as the ME analyzed them. Cowell was staring stoically straight ahead, obviously avoiding looking at the victims and the deep wounds on their heads.

Sadie made herself look, and not just so that she could see what the ME was telling her for herself. Madeline and Lydia deserved for their deaths to be witnessed, to be treated like people, not like slabs of flesh to be dissected and discussed as though they were in a lab. Sadie thought that was important when dealing with homicide victims like this. Making a connection with who the victim had been in life could help join the dots on a case better than a cooler detachment, in Sadie's experience. There was an emotional cost, but it was something that she had learned to bear.

Just about, anyway.

There was a large part of her that wanted to find the monster that had done this as quickly as possible so that she could tear him apart with her bare hands.

She felt the same way about Jessica's killer.

"There is a small defensive mark on this victim's body," the ME said, pointing to the inside of Madeline's forearm. That indicates she might have tried to fight him off, but briefly. This was not a prolonged struggle."

"There's nothing on Lydia's body," Sadie noticed.

The ME nodded curtly. "No," he agreed. "I would say the younger victim was taken by surprise. The placement of the wounds suggest that she was hit from behind, whereas it seems clear with the older one that she saw it coming and attempted to defend herself."

"She tried to save her own life," Cowell said quietly next to her. It was the first time he had spoken inside the morgue. "And she lost." He sounded angry.

The two women looked vulnerable and pale. They'd had their whole lives ahead of them, and now this faceless killer had ripped them away. It was the most violent, cowardly action she could imagine.

Sadie let out a slow exhale, letting the anger that she felt cool and crystallize into something hard and determined. She would find whoever did this, she vowed, no matter what it took.

Her phone buzzed in her pocket, and Sadie checked it with a mixture of relief and trepidation. Relief at being potentially called away from the morgue, but fear of it being Cooper and the news he would bring. But it wasn't Cooper; it was the number that Detective Lopez had given her to reach them on.

"I need to take this," Sadie murmured, stepping outside, and taking deep gulps of the air. It was stale corridor air maybe, but it was a lot fresher than next to those bodies.

"Agent Price," she answered.

"Hello Agent," Lopez said politely. "We've had a sighting of the girls come in from a truck stop just outside of Fairbanks; the last one the girls would have stopped at before...well, before the actual last one." Lopez paused before continuing. "We've just left the aunt and uncle's house, so you're nearer than we are. Do you want to go and take a look? Technically, it's just out of our jurisdiction."

"Yes, thank you," Sadie said, surprised but pleased that the two police officers were willing to share their information with her. Perhaps the historic wariness between local cops and feds was starting to break down.

Or perhaps the two officers were just more than happy to pass this particular case on.

"I'll take Cowell with me," she added before ringing off.

Cowell seemed more than happy to get away from the morgue, too.

*

The second truck stop was bigger and busier, with a proper shop and somewhere to eat. Sadie felt a rush of adrenalin that someone might have seen not just the girls but also their killer.

The sighting had been reported by the cashier in the one-stop shop, who waved them into the back when he saw them approaching the cashier desk. The back room was more like a cupboard, and as they crowded in Sadie felt uncomfortably aware of Cowell's thigh touching hers.

Cowell showed the cashier, a young guy barely out of his teens himself, the ID they had for the two girls. He stared at the pictures for a long time before nodding, looking distressed.

"Yes, they're the same girls. The blonde one, I noticed her because she was so pretty." He sounded almost as though he was about to cry. The alert that had gone out on the radio hadn't released the exact details of the girls' deaths, but it would be a shock to anyone, least of all a young man, to discover the girl he had been admiring the night before had turned up brutally murdered.

"Did you speak to them, beyond taking the money for whatever they bought? Did they buy anything?" Sadie was aware that she was peppering him with questions, but she felt an urgency to this case that had her on edge. Looking at the sisters lying dead on the ME's slab, it had been impossible not to keep thinking of herself and Jessica. Of all the times they had spoken about hitchhiking their way across the state to get away from their violent, alcoholic father. Jessica had been the sensible one who had said no, it was too dangerous. Clearly, she had been right.

But sensible or not, Jessica hadn't even made it to Madeline's age.

"They bought water and some snack bars. I asked them if they were hitchhiking – I mean, you could kinda tell, with the backpacks and everything. They said yes, and the blonde one, she seemed to want to chat, but the other girl hushed her, and they left. They seemed like they were running away from something, not just traveling. They had that look, you know?"

Sadie did know, all too well. "Did they say where they were headed?"

The cashier shook his head.

"Okay," Sadie said, trying not to show her disappointment that the visit hadn't yielded more information. At least, they could start tracking the girls' journey, and now they knew the killer had picked them up between here and the bathroom where they had been killed. That would be good for timings.

"What time was this?" Cowell asked, right on cue.

"I'm not sure...around eleven at night? I'm on a sixteen-hour shift. The security footage has the time on," he said apologetically.

"That was going to be my next question," Sadie said, smiling encouragingly at him. "Can you show us?"

There was a small TV and DVD player on the wall of the tiny room, and the cashier put it on, rewinding to the night before. At eleven-ten pm, the girls could be seen going into the shop. At eleven-twenty, they went out again.

"Do you have a camera outside?" Sadie asked.

"Yes, to watch the oil pumps. You can see a little way down the highway too." The cashier skipped to the right screen and Sadie and Cowell leaned forward simultaneously as they saw the girls passing the pumps and walking off down the side of the road. Just before they got out of sight they stopped, and the younger one started sticking her thumb out. A few moments later, a tanker came into view. It pulled up next to the girls.

"There!" Sadie said excitedly. "Pause the video."

The younger girl – Lydia, Sadie reminded herself – could be seen stepping forward and talking to the driver, then looking back to her sister. Madeline stood watching her sister climb aboard, clearly the more hesitant one, before she joined her. The driver couldn't be seen, and the number plate and ID of the tanker were fuzzy. The footage could be cleaned up, but that would slow them down. Sadie cursed to herself.

"I've got my laptop," Sadie told Cowell. "I can send the footage through to the Field Office in Anchorage – it will be quicker than sending it to Fairbanks PD, while we drive to Fairbanks to catch up with Lopez and Johnson."

Cowell nodded, happy for her to take the lead. The cashier took the disc from the player and handed it to Sadie without needing to be asked. He showed them back through the shop, not speaking until they reached the door.

"I hope you catch him," he said in heartfelt tones.

"So do I," Sadie said grimly, "so do I."

CHAPTER FIVE

Sadie sped south towards Fairbanks, her eyes on the road ahead of her but her mind on the case. The way Lydia had so carelessly climbed aboard the tanker, no doubt thinking they were lucky to get their next ride so quickly, having no idea what awaited them. It was a sad image, but it was preferable to the sight of them dead, posed in the bathroom stall where they had been found. That would be one of the images that stayed on Sadie's mind for a long time.

Next to her Cowell was quiet, and Sadie wondered if he was usually so reticent, or if the morning's events were getting to him.

"Have you seen anything like this before?" he said eventually, confirming her latter suspicions.

"Not exactly like this," she said with a sigh, "but if you're asking whether I've seen cases of young women being murdered, then sadly yes. In fact, I've seen too damn much of it."

Cowell shook his head. "You study the behavior of these psychos as well, don't you?"

"Before I got reassigned to Alaska, I was with the Behavioral Analysis Unit, yes," Sadie agreed. "But honestly, I still don't feel I understand what drives these people. I might know a lot about behavioral traits and patterns, and sometimes be able to predict a killer's next move, but in terms of really understanding how they can do what they do? It still baffles me."

"Pure evil," Cowell said darkly, raising a hand to his neck. Sadie quickly glanced across and saw he had pulled a crucifix from under his collar and was fiddling with it while staring out of the window.

"You're a Catholic?" she asked, feeling intrigued. Her parents had rarely gone to the local Baptist church, and Sadie was agnostic.

"Yeah," Cowell said heavily. "But I reckon I'm more scared of the kind of person that can do *that* than I am of any devil."

Me too, Sadie thought, then was startled by her phone ringing. Immediately on edge, she turned on her hands-free. But it still wasn't Cooper. It was the ME from back at the morgue.

"We have some initial conclusions," he told her, his voice as flat as it had been in person. "The wounds on their head killed them instantly.

Very deep, very damaging. The killer, whoever he is, is right-handed from the angle of the blows."

"That's good to know," Sadie said. Any clue was helpful. Left-handed would have been more helpful still, but she acknowledged they weren't likely to get so lucky.

"Any guidelines on height? Strength?"

"No, I can't give an estimate on height. The blows are very accurate. Using a heavy object accurately, it could be anyone of average strength. It wouldn't have taken someone exceptionally strong."

"And the toxicology?"

"Toxicology report hasn't come back yet. It'll probably take a few more days even if we prioritize it, but I don't see a reason to do that. Do you?"

Sadie shook her head. She didn't see a reason, and from all the evidence so far, and the signs of a brief struggle, it didn't seem likely the girls had been drugged at the time of death.

"We're still waiting to see if we can retrieve any DNA from Madeline. There's a small chance she might have something under her fingernails after trying to defend herself. As soon as we have results, I'll get them sent over to you."

"Thank you," Sadie said, but the ME had already ended the call, clearly in a rush to get back to his grisly workload. She concentrated on the seemingly endless road ahead, feeling frustrated. It was good of the ME to let her know his conclusions had been confirmed, and a few details on the perpetrator, but she hadn't learned anything groundbreakingly new.

Her phone rang again just moments after the call from the ME. Had he forgotten something? He had seemed pretty thorough.

"Agent Price? It's O'Hara. I've been processing the footage you sent over."

"Already?" Sadie was impressed. Agent O'Hara was Anchorage FBI's youngest recruit, and after working her last two cases with him, Sadie was certain he had a brilliant future.

"It was a simple enough job. It was a Shell tanker out of Prudhoe Bay; I'm guessing it was on its way to Anchorage. We can't get records from the DMV on who was driving it last night from the number plate alone, but you're in luck."

Sadie felt her heart speeding up.

"Why?"

"The tanker must have parked up for the night because it didn't get too far. It's just been processed at a weigh station near Denali State Park."

"I'm only a few miles from that turn," Sadie said, hitting the gas pedal.

"Well, if you take that turn and speed up, you might be able to catch him; he might not have left the weigh station yet," O'Hara said. "Even if he has, if you stop at the weigh station, they will be able to identify the driver. Although you might lose some time. Your call."

"Thanks, O'Hara," Sadie said. She glanced at Cowell and nodded in satisfaction.

"We might have just got our first breakthrough," she said.

Then she turned on the sirens.

*

Sadie all but ran into the weigh station, Cowell close behind her. She hadn't spotted the tanker but getting the identity of the driver was important. The scale operator looked up in surprise as Sadie headed straight for him, flashing her badge.

"FBI. Agent Price. Do you have the name of the driver whose Shell tanker was processed here about thirty minutes ago? And where it was headed?"

The operator looked taken aback.

"Well, this is unusual," he said. "Do you have a warrant?"

Sadie groaned inwardly, wondering if stopping here had been a mistake after all. But the assumption that the tanker was headed for Anchorage could have been wrong, and then Sadie would have taken the wrong turning and she and Cowell would be off on a wild goose chase.

"This is a murder investigation," she said bluntly. "We have no time to waste."

The scale operator looked reluctant, but nevertheless went to fetch the record, although he took his time leafing through the pages, seeming almost annoyed to have been bothered by them. Sadie bounced on her heels, impatient to be back on the road and in potential pursuit of the killer.

"Any chance of you doing that a bit faster?" Cowell said pointedly. The operator glared at him, but he did seem to speed up.

"Here we are," he said eventually, showing Sadie the log. "Clyde Rollins. Heading to Anchorage."

"Thank you," Sadie said over her shoulder, already racing back out to her truck. She was pulling away as soon as Cowell had shut the passenger door, the sirens back on and her foot pressing the gas pedal down as far as it would go.

"Can you call Fairbanks PD? Run Clyde's name through the database and see if he's got a record."

Cowell nodded and pulled out his cell, barking Clyde's details into his handset. Sadie listened, but she couldn't hear the voice on the other end of the line and so she had to wait until Cowell had finished his call.

"He's clean," he said, sounding frustrated. "Not a thing. Not even a parking violation."

"Doesn't necessarily mean anything," Sadie said. There were plenty of killers that she had arrested with no previous record. Perhaps the most harrowing case she had ever worked was her final one in Washington, D.C., when she had caught – and killed – the Boston Mangler. So-called because his first two victims had been in Boston, and because of the state their bodies had been left in. He had used power tools. And his record, too, had been squeaky clean. Sadie shuddered at the memory.

"But don't killers like this tend to build up to it?" Cowell asked, sounding interesting. "Like, you would expect them to start with just assault, maybe?"

"Yes, that's usually the case," Sadie acknowledged. "But the problem is, they don't always get caught. Serial killers are often among the more intelligent and cunning members of society."

Cowell looked taken aback. He was about to say something else when Sadie's phone rang yet again. This time, she was expecting it to be O'Hara or the ME again, and so when Cooper's voice came over the hands-free it gave her a jolt.

"Cooper. I'm in the car with State Trooper Cowell," she said quickly, letting him know that they were being overheard. There was a long pause, and Sadie knew exactly what the sheriff was about to tell her. She held her breath, and for a moment the current chase was all but forgotten as she thought back to the skeleton that they had discovered just hours before. How small it had seemed, crouched in the mineshaft, that for a moment Sadie had thought it must belong to a child.

Until she had seen the necklace.

Mother Dawn.

"I'll call you back," Cooper said.

"No!" Sadie said it too quickly, and she felt rather than saw Officer Cowell stare at her, surprised at her tone. "I mean," she said, modifying her tone, "that I really need to know the results of that particular case now. Right now," she added for emphasis, in case Cooper didn't get the point. She knew that he wouldn't want to tell her without being there to comfort her, but she didn't have time for noble gestures right now. She needed to know.

"Otherwise," she said, "I'll be wondering about it. And it will distract me from the current murder inquiry."

"You're sure?" Cooper sounded too hesitant. He wasn't going to tell her. Even though Sadie knew that he would only be acting this way if it was bad news, she still needed to hear him say it.

"Please, Cooper," she said quietly.

She heard him suck in his breath, and then there was another painful silence. She wondered if Cooper was still debating whether or not to tell her or was just choosing his words carefully so as not to reveal her personal information.

It turned out to be the latter.

"Okay," Cooper said with a heavy sigh. "The body that we found in the shaft. It belonged to Mother Dawn."

For a moment Sadie's vision went blurry, the road in front of her a hazy line. There was a loud buzzing in her ears.

Mother Dawn. Dawn Price.

Sadie's mother.

She had been murdered.

CHAPTER SIX

This devastating news was what she had been dreading to hear. Cutting the call, Sadie did her best to focus on the road ahead, gripping the wheel as she continued with their breakneck pursuit of the tanker. But meanwhile, her thoughts raced, filled with anguish.

Sadie had feared, as soon as they had found the skeleton, that it had belonged to her mother. Even without the necklace, carved with the name her Inuit patients had given her, Sadie had felt sure it was her.

But hearing it, and having it confirmed, somehow made it more real, and meant that she had to face it. Face the fact that not just her sister but her mother had been murdered. How could that be fair? A voice screamed inside her, the voice of a young girl who had been left with no one who cared about her. To lose her mother at only eight, and then her adored older sister seven years later? How could chance possibly be so cruel?

If it was chance.

Although Dawn and Jessica's deaths were far enough apart that they seemingly had nothing to do with each other, Sadie wasn't so sure. The deaths were different too. Sadie's mother had been shot. Jessica had been drowned in the frozen lakes, her death ruled originally as inconclusive.

Except, when he had originally called the local police to report his daughter missing, her father had said *"They* took her." He had denied it later.

Who were *they*? It had been haunting Sadie ever since. Why hadn't he admitted to this? What else was he keeping from her?

Then, when her father had been dying in the hospital, after Sadie had begged him to tell her what he knew about her sister's death, he had drawn her a map. She had assumed that whatever it led to would tell her about Jessica.

Instead, it had led to her mother's body. Sadie remembered her mother having cancer, and so for a long while had assumed that was what killed her. She had been too young to go to a funeral, and so for years had assumed her mother's disappearance was no more than her eventual succumbing to the tumors that were eating away at her.

Sadie had come back to Alaska intending to uncover some family secrets, but she had never expected this. She wanted to leave, to go home, to hide away as she battled to process this shock.

But she couldn't, not when a killer was out there, and lives were on the line.

"Agent Price! Over there!"

Sadie was jerked back to her current reality by Cowell's shout, and she followed the direction of his hand as he waved ahead and to the right.

In the distance, in the lane across from them, they could see an oil tanker that, as far as she could tell, looked a lot like the one on the security camera footage. Sadie crossed lanes and turned on her sirens again, speeding up even more in an attempt to catch up. She had to focus now! They were chasing down a suspected killer, and the agony she felt over her past would have to be pushed aside.

"You think it's him?" Cowell was leaning forward in his seat, straining against the belt.

"We'll soon find out," Sadie said, her eyes now glued to the tanker. As they got closer, her own heart started thumping wildly. It was the right number plate. Clyde Rollins was driving that tanker, and right now he was their number one – in fact, their only – suspect.

They were gaining rapidly on the oil tanker. Rollins must be able to see them by now, Sadie thought, turning on the flashers to indicate that she wanted him to pull over. But instead, the oil tanker sped up.

"He's not seriously going to try and make a run for it?" Cowell said disbelievingly. "Not in that thing."

"We'll cut him off," Sadie said confidently, her foot as hard on the gas as it could be. The tanker showed no signs of slowing but instead sped up more.

"He must be our guy," Cowell said. "Innocent men don't run."

"You'd be surprised. Everyone's guilty of something." Sadie came up alongside the tanker, and Cowell started gesturing for it to pull over. Rollins had to be able to see them in his wing mirror, but he obviously had no intentions of doing as they asked.

"Woah!" Cowell went white as the tanker suddenly swerved to the side, nearly grazing the side of their vehicle as though he was threatening to run them off the road. Sadie pressed her lips together angrily. Rollins wasn't just trying to run; he was now being actively aggressive.

"Idiot," she said, shaking her head. "If he crashes, that tanker could go up in flames. He'll kill himself before anyone else."

"He must be pretty desperate then," Cowell said. They were parallel with the driver's cab of the tanker now, and Sadie risked a glance at Rollin's profile. He was middle-aged and jowly with a receding hairline and pockmarked cheeks, and his eyes seemed to almost be bulging out of their sockets as he gripped the steering wheel, staring at the road ahead, resolutely ignoring them.

"He can't seriously think he's going to get away."

"He's panicking," Sadie said. "But we'll be able to overtake him just up ahead where the road bends. He will have to lose speed; he's driving an oil tanker, not a Ferrari."

Sure enough, at the bend Sadie was able to pull out in front of the tanker, leaving Rollins with little choice but to slam on his brakes. The tanker skidded, and Sadie gripped the wheel, watching carefully in her mirrors as he finally, reluctantly, slowed.

Suspecting he might make a run for it on foot, Sadie jumped quickly out of the police truck, her hand on her gun and Cowell behind her. They both ran for different sides of the cab in case he tried to get away, but instead Rollins didn't move. He kept his hands on the wheel, staring ahead as Sadie banged on the door. Slowly, he looked at her and then rolled down the window.

"Clyde Rollins." A statement rather than a question. The man shrugged, aiming for nonchalance although Sadie could see from the pulse in his jaw and the sheen of sweat on his brow that he was full of nerves.

"Who's asking?"

"I am," Sadie said curtly. "Special Agent Price, Anchorage FBI. My colleague here is State Trooper Cowell. We need to ask you a few questions."

Rollins's eyes had widened as she announced her name and rank, but he tried to keep up his façade even though it was slipping fast. "Ask away," he said, shrugging again. The effect would have been better if sweat wasn't now rolling into his bushy eyebrows.

"We'd prefer to ask you down at Fairbanks police department."

Rollins hesitated, but realizing he had no choice he opened his door and started to climb out of the cab.

"Hands in the air," Sadie barked as Cowell came around from the other side to join her. She drew her gun as Clyde Rollins stepped down from the truck, his hands in the air. He stared at it, and in spite of his fear a look of fury crossed his face. He didn't like being challenged, Sadie noted. Perhaps especially by a woman. That would certainly fit the profile of a killer who targeted young, defenseless women.

"What's this about?"

"Agent Price is asking the questions," Cowell said, eyeing the man with a look of distaste. "All you need to do is answer them."

"Not answerin' nothin' without a lawyer." Rollins sounded surly now. He started to lower his hands.

"In the air!" Sadie shouted. "Lower them again and you'll be lying on the ground."

"You can't arrest me," he protested. "I ain't done nothin'."

"Apart from speeding up instead of pulling over, and then trying to run us off the road, you mean?" Cowell said, sarcasm dripping from his voice.

"I didn't see you. It's windy," Cowell muttered. Sadie didn't bother to mention that the air, though freezing, was perfectly still.

"Did you pick up two young girls last night, Clyde?" Sadie asked, her tone almost conversational now. "Hitchhikers, at a stop outside of Fairbanks."

The man's eyes darted from left to right rapidly, but he didn't reply.

"It would be better for you if you told us the truth," Sadie offered helpfully, "especially since we have your vehicle recorded on camera."

Rollins seemed to deflate at her words, his shoulders and jowls sagging. "Yeah, okay, I did pick two girls up. They were standing in the cold. I couldn't leave them there, could I?"

"What happened to them after you picked them up?" Cowell was looking at Rollins as though he wanted to beat the man's brains out. The state trooper could be a hothead, Sadie guessed. A lot like her when she had started out.

"How would I know? I didn't take them far. Then I dropped them off."

"You dropped them off? Where?"

"I don't remember. It was a small rest stop. I have no idea which one."

Was he keeping the details deliberately vague because he knew that the evidence would point to him as the killer, Sadie wondered. At any rate, Clyde Rollins was looking more and more guilty by the minute. Sadie raised an eyebrow at him. "Why did you not take them far? I'm guessing they wanted to get all the way to a city, not to a rest stop."

The man shrugged, but he looked panicked again. "I don't have to answer your questions," he said. "If those girls are in trouble, it's got nothin' to do with me. I knew they were trouble, that's why I dropped them off."

"What did they do to make you think they were in trouble? Did they make you angry, Mr. Rollins?"

He glared at her, his anger coming to the fore again. "What have they said? They're probably lying to you," he stated, and Sadie threw a quick glance at Cowell. Did he really not know they were dead, or was he just a good actor? Sadie had a feeling he was more intelligent than he let himself appear. A sort of low cunning, at least.

"Haven't you been listening to your radio, Mr. Rollins?" She paused and then said slowly so as to let her words sink in, "They're dead."

For a moment Rollins seemed to freeze, then he did something that Sadie wouldn't have expected, given that she still had her gun trained on him. He feinted to the side towards Cowell, then as Sadie pivoted towards him, he ran the opposite way, as if to get around the other side of the truck.

But Sadie was a trained agent, and she was fast. She sprinted in pursuit, firing a warning shot as she did so, and it startled him enough that he tripped and landed heavily on the asphalt. Sadie was on him in seconds, cuffing his hands behind his back as he lay panting on the ground. Cowell dragged him to his feet by his arm, his gun trained on him, as Sadie got up, replaced her gun, and dusted herself off.

"That was a very silly thing to do, Mr. Rollins," he said, his voice laced with anger, "because now we can bring you in for obstruction and resisting arrest."

"I want a lawyer," Rollins said sulkily as Cowell pushed him into the back of his truck, pushing his head forward so he didn't bang it on the top of the doorframe.

"You drive," Cowell said, "I'll sit in the back with him." He didn't sound as though he relished the prospect. Sadie nodded and got back into the front of the vehicle, turning it around and heading back the way they had come. "We'll go to the nearest state station," she told Cowell. "Fairbanks will be too far." She didn't want to completely retrace their steps. Clyde Rollins hadn't traveled far thanks to his overnight stop, but he had still come far enough that he could easily have driven past more vulnerable women on the side of the road.

An image of the way that the girls' bodies had been dumped in the restroom stall swam into her mind and Sadie shuddered, glancing back at Rollins in the rear-view mirror. He had his head down and his hands cuffed behind his back, but he still managed to exude an air of menace. Had he done that to Madeline and Lydia, leaving them there for another woman to find?

As she had the thought, Clyde Rollins's eyes met hers in the mirror and in spite of his defeated posture, he glared at her with unabashed fury. Sadie raised a cool eyebrow but inside she felt shaken. She took her eyes back to the road, thinking of the crime scene again.

In her experience, a killer who could go to those lengths wouldn't be happy with just one kill. He would want more, and that cruel appetite would grow.

Sadie had a horrible feeling that there were more bodies out there. And that it was going to be up to her to find them.

CHAPTER SEVEN

Clyde Rollins sat across from Sadie in the tiny interrogation room, glowering at her and Cowell from under heavy eyelids. His beefy arms were crossed over his belly and in spite of the cold there was the smell of acrid sweat coming from him, rolling across the metal table towards them. Sadie wrinkled her nose.

Two police officers had been dispatched to search Rollins's tanker, while they embarked on the vital job of questioning this unwilling suspect.

There was an undoubtable air of menace emanating from him.

From the way he looked at her, Sadie could tell that he didn't respect her at all. Perhaps that was why, after half an hour, they had not yet made any headway with the questioning.

So far, Rollins was just stubbornly repeating his story that he had picked up the sisters from the rest stop and dropped them off at another location further on. He was refusing to elaborate on details, and both Sadie and Cowell were getting more and more frustrated.

"There must be a reason," Cowell said through gritted teeth, "why you left them there? You were going in the same direction. Why did you suddenly drop them off?"

Rollins yawned and shifted in his seat, prompting a fresh wave of body odor. "They wanted to be dropped off. I dunno why. How many times do I need to tell you the same thing?"

"You said earlier they were trouble. Now you are saying they wanted to be dropped off? Why?" Sadie immediately picked up the inconsistency in the versions.

"Look, they were trouble, coming at me with these demands that they wanted to get out. So I did what they asked."

"And you don't remember where you stopped? How's that even possible?" Sadie pressured.

"Because I was listening to music. I was doing my thing. I wasn't speaking to them."

"Then how did you know they were trouble?"

"Two girls like that on their own, you know it's going to be that way. I didn't kill them. I'm sorry they're dead. But I don't know how it happened," Rollins protested, now looking sorry for himself.

Sadie tapped her fingernails on the table, giving him a smile that had no humor in it. "What's bothering me," she told him slowly, "is it's a big coincidence. And I don't like coincidences; they make me suspicious. You're asking us to believe that you dropped the girls at a stop you can't remember, for no apparent reason, and the next thing, someone else came along and murdered them? Surely you can see our problem here. You're right in the frame, Mr. Rollins."

Rollins continued to look scared but he tried to hide it, looking away and shrugging. "That's what I told you," he insisted. "Not my fault if they got themselves into trouble after I left them."

"Got themselves into trouble?" Cowell repeated, outraged by Rollins's comment. "Is that what you call it?"

Sadie tipped her head to one side as she watched their suspect. Something about the way he had phrased his last comment made her think.

"What makes you assume they were troublemakers, Clyde?" she asked. "As opposed to victims? That's how most people would respond when hearing about murder, surely?"

"Most innocent people, anyway," Cowell added. That seemed to tip Rollins over the edge. He jumped to his feet, spittle flying from his mouth. "I told you I had nothin' to do with it!"

Cowell and Sadie were both on their feet in an instant, with Cowell looking more than ready to leap over the table and fell Rollins with one punch. "Sit your ass down," he snarled, "or I'll sit it down for you."

"You can't threaten me," Rollins grumbled, but he sat down anyway. Sadie followed suit, deliberately taking a few moments to get herself comfortable, while Cowell sat ramrod straight in his chair, glaring at Rollins. Cowell was a hothead, Sadie realized, much as she had been as a newer agent, and it was a trait that could be an asset or a hindrance, depending on the particular case and suspect.

Rollins sudden outburst had surprised Sadie, although perhaps it shouldn't have considering his actions when they had tried to apprehend him in his tanker. He obviously had a temper, perhaps enough to lash out and kill the Heard girls.

"You've got a bit of a temper there, I see," she said sweetly. "Did Madeline and Lydia make you angry too?"

Rollin's leg was juggling with either temper or nerves: probably both. "I didn't hurt them," he protested once more. "You're trying to pin this on me just because was in the wrong place at the wrong time. I was offering them a ride. I didn't have to."

"How very gentlemanly of you," Cowell said sourly. It was obvious to Sadie that the state trooper didn't believe a word that Clyde Rollins said and that he thought the driver was guilty. Sadie wasn't entirely sure, but she knew there was something that he wasn't telling them and judging by the way he spoke about the sisters, she thought that she had guessed what it was.

"It was helpful of you," she agreed, earning a puzzled glance from Cowell. "A lot of people wouldn't have picked them up, especially two teenagers. They could have robbed you right there on the road, you know."

"That's right," Rollins said, looking relieved at Sadie's sudden change of tone. "I was just trying to do my duty. It was obvious they were running from something, two young girls like that."

Sadie nodded along, smiling at him. "Were they rude to you, Mr. Rollins? Or mean? Is that why you dropped them off? Maybe they weren't grateful enough for all of your help?"

Rollins stiffened in his chair and Sadie knew that she had guessed correctly as his piggy little eyes moved rapidly from side to side.

"What you getting at now?" he mumbled, but he couldn't meet her eyes. Next to her, Cowell leaned forward, picking up on Sadie's train of thought.

"No one would blame you if you expected a little...kindness...in return for your own help, you know what I mean?" Cowell raised his eyebrows suggestively and Rollins flinched.

"That's it, isn't it," Cowell said, his tone switching back to one of disgust. "You expected sexual favors from them, and they refused."

"Is that why you killed them, Mr. Rollins?" Sadie followed up, her voice deceptively soft even though she was bracing herself for another outburst from the guy. Instead, Rollins seemed to crumple in his seat, his jowls and belly sagging.

"I swear, I didn't kill them," he said, sounding as though he was about to cry.

"But you did expect something from them," Sadie pressed. Rollins looked ashamed now, his face red as he stared down at his shoes.

"There's nothing wrong with that," he mumbled. "A lot of working girls hang 'round down that stretch of road, how was I supposed to know? And you don't get nothing for free in this world," he finished, a little more defiantly. "Yes, I asked them, but they said no. They got mad at me for asking. So I dropped them at the next stop. That's all."

Sadie didn't answer, letting his words linger in the air. It was Cowell who spoke first, again sounding as though he was holding himself back from body slamming Rollins to the ground.

"So, what you're telling me and Agent Price here," he said, "is that you thought you were going to get sex from them, and when they obviously refused, you dropped them off at the truck stop you don't remember, and left them there?"

"That's it," he said.

"But why bother to drop them there?" Sadie said, thinking through the potential holes in his story. "If you were so annoyed that they wouldn't give you what you wanted, then why didn't you just drop them at the side of the road?"

"Because I wouldn't do that! Not to anyone, not in this weather. Being by the side of the road in this season, you could die if a storm blew in. Look, I was mad at them. I thought they'd led me on. But when they said no, I respected it. I just wasn't going to take them further," he protested. "Maybe they walked further to look for a ride. There was a bigger stop a few miles up ahead, that I do know."

Cowell's nose wrinkled as though there was a bad smell – or rather, a worse stench than the one that Rollins was already giving off.

"I'm telling the truth," Rollins insisted, looking imploringly at Sadie now. "I didn't kill them. Why would I?"

Although she couldn't be sure and he certainly remained their chief suspect, Sadie felt inclined to believe him. Not because she thought Rollins had an ounce of compassion in him for either of the girls but because his story did, in a twisted way, make sense. She could see him as a molester, certainly, but she wasn't convinced he had killed them. If this personality type had murdered, Sadie would have expected to see more evidence of assault. Of abuse. Even of rape. That hadn't happened in this case. Apart from the head wounds, these kills had been clean.

But Cowell was clearly furious that Rollins had even tried to solicit the two young women.

"Are you impotent, Mr. Rollins?" he asked in a derogatory way. "Do you try your luck with random women in case they can help you?"

"Huh?" He looked as though he didn't understand the word.

"Can't get hard," Cowell supplied helpfully. "I mean, you're carrying a few extra pounds there, and you're sitting down a lot in your line of work. Unhealthy. Not good for performance."

Rollins looked outraged. "No I am not! Why you asking me that? You're harassing me now! This is sexual harassment from the police!"

"Don't flatter yourself," Cowell said, sounding like he was starting to enjoy himself.

There was a tap at the door, and Sadie saw the face of one of the police officers at the glass. She excused herself, letting herself quietly out of the interrogation room and hoping that Cowell could contain himself from baiting Rollins any further. She could see he was mad at the trucker, but insulting him and going off on a tangent wouldn't be helpful. He was clearly not going to get angry enough to spill any of the information they needed – mostly because Sadie now doubted he possessed that information at all.

"We just had word back from the guys at the tanker," the young cop told her. "And they found something."

"What did they find?" Sadie felt adrenaline surge. Was this going to be proof that Rollins was, in fact, their killer?

"They found a log book that shows the truck is linked to a tracking system. Being an oil tanker owned by a big supplier, it's monitored en route. They got in touch with the online tracking company and they just sent the plan of the route. The truck didn't stop at all at the place where the two victims were found. It stopped about fifty miles earlier, at a very small truck stop that was little more than a gas station. That's where he must have let them out. So they might have picked up another ride after that."

"Thanks. It's good to have that confirmed," Sadie nodded, realizing that although she was disappointed, she wasn't surprised. She was becoming more and more convinced that Clyde Rollins wasn't their guy. He was a pervert and a creep, but she had already doubted he was the killer. She walked back into the interrogation room and sat down, eyeballing Rollins until he quivered.

"We've searched your vehicle," she told him, "The tracking record has cleared you, so you're free to go. But be careful who you pick up in the future, and what you ask from them. What you're doing is often how trouble starts, and turns bad quickly."

Looking relieved, Rollins nodded and got to his feet, a look of cockiness coming back to his face now that he realized he wasn't going to be charged. "Told you, I wasn't your man," he said with a self-satisfied smirk.

"Just one thing, Clyde," Sadie said. Rollins paused and looked at her. "What?"

"Even if you're not responsible for those girls being killed," she said, letting her own disgust for him now fully show in her voice, "In a way you may as well have killed them. Because if you hadn't been such a creep as to have left them stranded because they didn't want to have sex with you, they wouldn't have fallen prey to the murderer, would they? You might want to think about that before you go propositioning young women who are just trying to get a ride, and then abandoning them in the middle of nowhere."

Rollins looked sick as he hurried off. Sadie looked at Cowell and sighed, feeling suddenly exhausted. She had been up at the crack of dawn investigating the mine shaft, which now felt like days rather than hours ago.

She was trying not to think about that, though. She could only solve one murder at a time.

"So, now what? We're at a dead end," Cowell said gloomily.

"We'll speak to Johnson and Lopez and see what information they got from the girls' family about why they were running away. Most women are killed by someone they know – we can't rule that out just because we know they were hitchhiking."

They were both standing up to leave when Sadie got another call. It was Paul Golightly.

"Price," he greeted her, and at the sound of his tone she somehow knew immediately what he was about to tell her.

"Sir," she replied. "What is it?"

"You need to get yourself up to another rest stop, this one just north of Wasilla," he said. "I'll send you the coordinates."

Sadie hesitated as her stomach sank. "You mean...?"

"Yes," he said. "There's been another body found."

CHAPTER EIGHT

The victim was alone, Sadie realized, as she arrived at the scene, which was already being attended to by police. She walked inside the restroom feeling angry and afraid that this killer was so far ahead, leaving a trail of death behind.

This woman had been left in the men's stall rather than the women's, dumped on the floor face up, like the Heard sisters. Just one woman, this time, but that didn't make Sadie feel any better. Three bodies in a matter of hours? Situations like this could only make her think of one question.

How many more?

Sadie inspected the body, being careful not to disturb or touch the crime scene before forensics had arrived to process it. This woman, a blonde who looked to be early thirties, was different than the Heard sisters. She was emaciated, with obvious track marks on the inside of her arms and bad teeth. A heroin addict, which meant she could well be a sex worker who had been hanging around the truck stop looking for business. The Wasilla rest stop was known for it, Cowell had told Sadie on the way.

What a waste of a life, Sadie thought sadly, *to then end up like this*. Looking at the deep, and clearly fatal head wound, she could see it was the same modus operandi as before.

She had been wearing a low-cut, ragged sweater, and all Sadie could think was how she must have been freezing, waiting in the cold for a lonely trucker to take her up on her potential offer of cheap sex.

"Looks like the same guy," Cowell said quietly next to her. His eyes were anywhere but on the dead woman.

Sadie nodded. They had a serial killer on their hands.

This rest stop had no cameras and a cursory look around outside revealed nothing. Unlike the sisters, there were no belongings to identify the victim more accurately. They had to hope that this time the forensics team or ME would find some DNA or other evidence.

Without speaking, Sadie stepped out of the men's bathroom, Cowell following. She wanted to talk to the maintenance guy, Rick. He was the person who had found the body and called it in. His first impressions might be important.

Rick was a wiry, dark-haired guy with a thick mustache, standing and fidgeting outside the stalls.

"Can I go now?" he asked. "I have other jobs to do."

Sadie eyed him suspiciously. He was anxious, and not meeting their eyes. Sure, he had just found a body and probably wasn't feeling his best, but she got the feeling he was a bit too keen to leave the crime scene.

"Local police are on their way," Sadie told him. "And they will need to speak with you too. Can you just run me through how you found the body?"

Rick looked annoyed. "I already said all this when I called it in."

"Well, you didn't say it to me," Sadie said. Rick sighed.

"Like I already said," he said, emphasizing the *already*, "I came in to do the cleaning and checks, went into the men's stall, and saw her. I phoned the cops straight away. I felt scared, finding her like that. I mean, I nearly threw up. I've never seen a body before."

"It must have been very distressing," Sadie said politely. Rick nodded, but Sadie thought that he didn't seem all that distressed, not for someone who had just walked in on a murder scene.

"And you don't recognize her?"

"Never saw her before in my life," Rick said, giving a sharp nod that made her aware of his slightly jutting chin.

"No one hanging around when you arrived, or a vehicle that could have been just leaving?" Cowell sounded impatient next to her, and Sadie understood the feeling. She hated the waiting for something to turn up, a concrete lead that she could chase down.

Especially when she felt as though the clock was ticking down for the next victim. She could be wrong, but these murders had all the hallmarks of a serial killer who had no intention of stopping anytime soon. Three bodies in twenty-four hours suggested the start of a spree. Of someone who had gotten the taste for killing and wasn't going to stop until he was satiated.

Or until Sadie stopped him.

"Nope, nothing," Rick said, sounding just as impatient himself. "There's nothing I can tell you, and I can't tell the Wasilla cops anything more either. I need to get going. You can't make me stay," he said defiantly. Sadie raised an eyebrow at him.

"No," she conceded, "I can't. But seeing as you were the first person on the scene, it won't look very good for you if you don't want to cooperate. We need to know who did this, Rick."

Rick looked mutinous, but didn't speak, leaning against the wall and folding his arms. Taking that as acquiescence that he wasn't about to go anywhere, Sadie walked down the length of the stop, motioning with her head for Cowell to follow her.

"Once the Wasilla police arrive," she said quietly, "we'll go around the nearest stops, see if anyone can ID the victim. Judging by her track marks there's a strong chance that she's a sex worker working the stops, so someone might recognize her."

"The killer's chosen a very different victim this time," Cowell said, nodding at her suggestion.

Sadie sighed. "Sadly, a lot of serials start with sex workers, even if they're not their 'ideal victim.' Due to the fact these people are often living under the radar and their disappearance is less likely to be noticed, they make easier targets. The public tends to care a lot less about women like this than victims like, say, the Heard sisters. It's a lot easier to have sympathy for two young women on the cusp of life than a drug addict."

"So, this could be just opportunistic?" Cowell said. "She just turned up, like the Heard sisters were just trying to hitch a lift?"

"Could be," Sadie said, thinking through the likely scenarios, "or maybe he deliberately targeted her. It could be her regular haunt. Maybe the sisters whet his appetite and so he headed here deliberately, knowing what he would find."

"You said sex workers get targeted because no one notices when they disappear," Cowell said, "But he wanted us to notice his one."

"Yes, he did," Sadie said in a grim tone. "Dumping them in a restroom, to be discovered, indicates a need for shock value and to brag about what he's done. But I wouldn't be surprised if he's killed before, building up to this. And sex workers and runaways are all likely victims. I'll have checks done for disappearances. For all we know, he could have been killing for years."

"Why?" Cowell sounded both fascinated and disgusted. "What makes someone do something so horrific to someone else?"

"Honestly? I don't know. I can give you all the theories and profiles, but when it comes down to it, there's no reason that makes any sense. Sometimes I feel like the more I do this job, the less I understand."

Cowell gave her an odd look and Sadie turned her face away, momentarily embarrassed. It wasn't like her to be so maudlin, but the combination of another body and the discovery that the bones were indeed her mother's had put her in a more reflective state of mind. She shook her head, telling herself to snap out of it. Focus on one thing at a time.

But she felt hot in spite of the weather, a wave of nausea and dizziness washing over her. It had been an intense day so far, and she couldn't remember the last time she had eaten. She excused herself to Cowell and made her way into the women's bathroom, intending to splash her face with cold water. She needed to stay concentrated on the task at hand.

In the smeared mirror above the single, cracked basin, Sadie saw how tired she looked. Her cheeks were hollow and there were rings under her eyes so dark that they looked like bruises. Her honey colored hair was escaping from its bun and her usually bright green eyes were dull.

You look like a zombie, Sadie Price, she told herself. At times like this, she had to wonder what Cooper saw in her.

In spite of her weariness, a half-smile tugged at her lips as she thought of Cooper and she saw her own face light up in the glass. Shaking her head at herself she splashed her face and fixed her hair. She was directly in front of one of the toilet stalls, its door wide open. As her eyes drifted to its reflection, Sadie spotted something, and then froze.

Was that blood on the floor?

Turning around, Sadie made her way carefully to the entrance of the stall and crouched down. Sure enough, there was blood both on the floor and the back of the cubicle, and it didn't look as though it had been there that long. Sadie had a strong suspicion that the blood would match the DNA of the latest victim.

That explained why she was in the men's bathroom this time. This was where the kill must have happened. And then, just as in the previous kills, the body had been moved.

Sadie strode out of the bathroom, nearly walking straight into Cowell's fist.

"Whoa!" Cowell exclaimed, jumping back as Sadie immediately went into a defensive stance, which in Sadie's case looked exactly the same as ready to attack. "I was trying to knock. Rick's gone."

"Gone?" Sadie ran towards the entrance to see the maintenance van speeding off down the highway. In the other direction a local cop car approached.

"Yeah, I tried to get him to stay but he refused. He said he was going home. He seemed panicked suddenly."

Sadie glared at the van as it receded into the distance, reaching for her phone.

"We need to get Rick's home address, and question him again," she told Cowell. "There was something off in the way he answered our questions. I'm wondering now if he moved the body himself. And that might mean he is the killer, too."

CHAPTER NINE

While Sadie waited impatiently for Cowell to call up Rick's address details, feeling sure that the maintenance man had played a part in this crime, the medical examiner arrived on the scene. The ME had arrived with a local cop, an older, gray-bearded guy who seemed a lot more hostile to Sadie's presence than the Fairbanks cops had. Sadie ignored him. This was a federal case now. She was much more interested in what the ME made of the body.

Like Sadie herself, once he took a look at the body and the evidence, the medical examiner was convinced that the body had been moved from the ladies' restroom to the men's. But he reiterated that they would need DNA confirmation on the blood before they could prove it conclusively.

"It doesn't mean it was Rick who killed her," Cowell pointed out.

"No," Sadie agreed, "it doesn't. But his responses seemed suspicious to me. His whole demeanor, for someone who had discovered a body like that, was off. I think there's something he's not telling us, and we need to find out what it is."

"You think he could be the killer?"

Sadie shrugged. "I'm not convinced, mostly because what he did seems too sloppy. Surely, he would have cleaned up properly before calling it in? But we can't rule it out; we need to question him. Let's see if anything comes back on his record before we get going."

Feeling sad, Sadie looked at the dead woman's face while the examiner worked, staring at the hollowed-out cheeks and prominent cheekbones, and wondered if she had anyone who would miss her, and who would care if she didn't come home.

Then Sadie's phone beeped and she checked it to see the information that she had requested on Rick had come through. She stepped out of the bathroom, leaving the ME to his job, and motioned for Cowell to follow her.

"New info?" the state trooper asked, almost bouncing on his heels with impatience. He was someone who preferred to be on the go rather than standing around at crime scenes; that much was evident. Sadie nodded.

"Yup. It seems our maintenance guy has got quite a history. He lives about thirty minutes away; I say we go and question him. There's enough here to bring him in for it."

Cowell raised an eyebrow. "What are his previous convictions?"

"Three counts of assault spanning the lass twelve years. The last one was a road rage conviction a year ago where a woman in another car was badly injured, although he only got two months' jail time for that. I wonder what that was about." She shook her head at the absurdity of the criminal justice system. As a federal agent, she knew there was nothing worse for anyone in law enforcement than to bring someone guilty in and watch them either get off or plea bargain their way out of an appropriate sentence. She wanted to know more about Rick's last conviction, but they didn't have time just now.

"Let's go," Cowell said. He was already walking towards the truck. Sadie pocketed her phone and followed him.

He climbed into the car. "It's an easy drive. Should be no traffic on the way. But it's not a good part of town," he said.

"You know this place well?" she asked.

Cowell ran a hand through his blonde hair. "Yes. Palmer was my local 'hood for a few years, before I joined law enforcement."

"What did you do before that?" Sadie asked.

"I wanted to be a professional musician, believe it or not. My friends and I formed a band. Being a very small town, and a close community, we got quite a few gigs. We played at a lot of the local venues and got to know the area well."

"A boy band?" Sadie almost burst out laughing. That had been her very first impression when she'd met Cowell, and it had turned out to be true? "And what did you do in the band?" she asked.

"Drummer, of course!" He grinned, his face warming, as if he felt pleased to be discussing a lighter topic than the murders. "I studied music at college, so I can also play guitar fairly well, and I'm an okay singer for backing vocals. It was fun for the year that it lasted. Then our lead singer got married and moved to Fairbanks. We followed him, but the band didn't do so well there, and we went our separate ways, and while I was deciding what to do, my folks suggested I join the police. My older brother is in law enforcement, in Minnesota. So I followed in his footsteps the year before last, at the age of twenty-three."

Sadie felt she knew her current partner a lot better, now that she had learned something about him. Studying music was not the usual road to working for the police, that was for sure. But now, knowing his background, she could understand more about the passionate and intense personality he'd shown. As they subsided into an easy silence, she found herself thinking about the crimes again, her mind returning relentlessly to the case. What kind of personality were they looking for? When they found this murderer, what would be the characteristics of this brutal killer?

Focusing on the road as they reached the town of Palmer and wound their way through the streets, she saw that they were approaching a rundown looking terrace on an equally rundown street that was home to a crumbling strip of houses, a filling station, and a shop that advertised ice fishing gear but looked as though it had been closed for a long time. This definitely was the wrong side of the tracks, in what she had seen otherwise to be a peaceful and scenic town.

There was no sign of the maintenance van outside of Rick's address.

"I suppose it would be too good to be true that he would have just gone home," Sadie said with a sigh as they approached the front door. "He knows we're going to want to question him after discovering the body was moved."

She pounded the front door, but as she expected there was no response. Meanwhile, Cowell peered through the grimy front windows.

"Can you see inside?"

"Yeah, and it looks empty. There's not even much furniture. I wonder if he even spends a lot of time here."

"A girlfriend, maybe," Sadie said, and then frowned as she thought of his record. She would bet good money that Rick was far from an ideal boyfriend.

"Didn't he say he inspected other restrooms?" Cowell said. "He might just have carried on working. Especially if he wants to claim innocence. Making a full-on run for it just makes him look guilty."

Sadie nodded. She was already reaching once again for her cell phone to call the maintenance company that Rick worked for. Sure enough, his schedule dictated that he should be inspecting another rest area, just outside of Palmer.

"Well, we're going in the right direction," Sadie commented as she got back into the vehicle. "So at least we haven't wasted too much time."

Cowell looked thoughtful, his brow creased with anxiety. "What is it?" Sadie asked.

"Nah, it would be too brazen," Cowell said, answering his own unspoken thoughts.

"What would?" Sadie asked as they pulled back out onto the highway, her tone impatient.

"Just, if Rick is the killer, and he's on some kind of spree like you said...do you think this next rest stop could be where he dumps his next victim?"

Sadie didn't answer.

But she did hit the gas.

CHAPTER TEN

She was perfect.

The rest area was another run down, deserted affair with little more than a bench and some toilets, and there was no one else around. As the watcher observed the scene, the woman in leather pants who had just pulled up on her motorcycle removed her helmet, revealing long, dyed red hair.

The watcher's mouth curled in distaste. What kind of woman went around flaunting herself like that? The bright hair and the too tight leather pants were practically begging for attention of the wrong sort. She was exposing herself. Asking for punishment.

And the watcher was just the person to give it to her.

It almost felt divinely ordained, the way these women just kept dropping like flies into a spider web, turning up at just the right times. Hang around long enough and the prey always presented themselves.

It was a good analogy, the spider, the watcher decided. Spiders weaved a web and then just patiently sat, watching and waiting, for the stupid little flies to crawl right into it. No hunting or chasing required.

There was some work needed here though, to ensure the woman didn't roar back off on the motorcycle too fast. Luckily, the watcher had some skill with engines.

The redheaded woman left her motorbike and walked across to the toilets, giving the watcher a chance to set the trap. To finish weaving the web for the woman to get stuck in.

It was important to move quickly. This prey was a little more challenging than the other kills, who really had just walked straight up and presented themselves. Those foolish sisters, little sluts the pair of them, especially the younger one, had climbed into the vehicle without a care in the world. As if the world owed them a living, in fact. They'd clearly been down and outs, the dregs of society, trying to catch a ride for free because they couldn't handle life. That was the impression they gave, and they had gotten what was coming to them.

As for the woman that morning, well, she had been a whore, a sad loser. Desperate and degenerate and willing to take any offer that came her way. To sell herself for a few bucks, maybe even the offer of food and shelter. Displaying herself to all comers. It was disgusting. Demeaning, in fact.

Putting that one out of her misery had been a mercy, really.

The redhead was just the same, trailing across the forecourt, looking downtrodden and discouraged. Clearly her life was going nowhere and she was on a losing streak.

She pushed back her red hair, as if making the gesture for the benefit of any watchers, even though there was of course, only one.

As the door closed behind the woman, the watcher knew it was time.

Disabling the motorcycle by cutting a few wires took seconds, but even so the watcher's heart thumped audibly while doing the work. This was the risky part, where this prey could discover the interference. Luckily, the woman took her time in the toilet and by the time she came out the watcher was safely back out of sight in the truck, and there was no indication that the motorcycle had been touched.

The redhead tried to start the engine a few times and then stopped and got off, looking frustrated. She crouched down to inspect her bike, looking perplexed.

The fly was in the middle of the web. Time to incapacitate her.

Clutching the tire iron, the watcher got out of the vehicle and walked towards this pretty, ignorant prey whose time had come.

"Hey, are you okay? Is there anything I can do to help?"

The woman looked up, saw the watcher, and immediately looked doubtful. How insulting that in a moment, this down-and-out woman with a broken bike didn't think the watcher could offer any value? In fact, her stare seemed derogatory.

"I don't think you can help, but thanks."

"Oh, I think I can."

The tire iron swung through the air.

CHAPTER ELEVEN

Sadie felt a knot of tension tightening inside her as they pulled up outside the rest area. Cowell's earlier words had gotten her thinking about the speed of these kills, and now she couldn't help fearing the worst.

"It looks pretty busy here," Cowell commented as they climbed out of the car. Sadie nodded, scouring the area for any sign of Rick's maintenance van. There were three camper vans with families, who all seemed to know each other, but no sign of Rick or his van. Feeling frustrated, Sadie walked toward the buildings.

"I'll check inside; you check the perimeter. Ask the parents if they've seen a maintenance man. You might want to warn them to keep their families close, too," she added, since a killer might be on the prowl.

Sadie went inside. This rest stop, like the one where she had questioned the cashier who had spoken to the Heard sisters, had a small shop and convenience store. However, she realized it was too busy to be a viable place to commit murder and dump a body, at least in the middle of the day, and Sadie found herself breathing a sigh of relief on that front. After Cowell's comment, she had convinced herself they were driving straight into another crime scene.

Three bodies in one day – four, if she counted her mother's bones – were too much even for an agent with Sadie's experience. She had to catch this perpetrator before number five showed up.

But was Rick their guy? If he had nothing to hide then he should be here, working. Unless they had just missed him. Sadie checked the toilets first, breathing another sigh of relief when all the stalls turned out to be empty. Then she went into the convenience store. The cashier was an older woman with short purple hair, who looked at Sadie with undisguised hostility when she introduced herself. It didn't faze Sadie. She had learned early on in her career that some people just didn't like law enforcement agents of any description.

"Do you know if the maintenance man, Rick Tuftner, has been here today? It's his day, right?"

The woman nodded but her expression remained sour. "It's supposed to be, yeah, but he's a lazy son of a bitch if you ask me. He doesn't ever seem to do anything, and some weeks he doesn't even bother to turn up. Beats me why he hasn't been fired yet."

Sadie thanked the cashier and went back outside to join Cowell, who shook his head. "He hasn't been seen," he told her. "Guess he's not gonna show up for work today."

"Or he could just be late," Sadie pointed out. "Let's get in the truck and wait a while and figure out our next move. I want to check his record on the computer as well and get more details on this kidnapping conviction."

"You think he's escalating, then?"

"Could be." There was no doubt that Rick's record showed a typical build-up pattern, even if two murders in one day was unprecedented. She wondered, if he was the killer, what had tipped him over the edge.

Back in the truck Sadie fired up her laptop and accessed the database, drumming her fingertips on her thigh impatiently as she waited for the information that she needed to load.

"Here we go." Sadie scanned the screen and sucked in her breath as she absorbed the information. "Look at this," she said, spinning the screen to show Cowell. "It seems the most recent victim he assaulted was an ex-girlfriend, Mary-Jane Preston, who was a few months away from her twentieth birthday at the time. He swore at her, slapped her in the face, and finally punched her hard enough to break two ribs, after they fought."

Cowell stared at the screen, looking confused. "And he only served a couple of months for that?"

"It seems like it was an abusive relationship. She changed her statement and said he hadn't punched her. Then they dated again, once he was out of jail."

"How the hell does that work?" Cowell swore, shaking his head. "So, she was his girlfriend, and she refused to state the full extent of the abuse? How does that work? How does anyone get to that stage?"

"It's classic abuser tactics. Seems she waited for him while he was in prison like a good little victim. He got under her skin." Sadie tried and failed to imagine what any woman would see in Rick. He must have a charm that Sadie had missed.

"So," Cowell said slowly. "Maybe he's living with Mary-Jane? That would explain why his own house seemed so bare. Should we try her address? It's in Palmer too, and not so far from here."

"That's exactly what I'm thinking," Sadie said. "Girlfriend or not, if Rick's predilection for assault has tipped over into outright murder, then Mary-Jane could be in serious danger."

*

Mary-Jane's apartment was in a slightly nicer part of town than Rick's house had been, on the ground floor of an apartment block with a small yard out front. A dog barked from one of the apartments as Sadie and Cowell approached. Although this was technically only an inquiry, Sadie held her hand near her gun.

There was no sign of Rick's maintenance van, but Sadie expected there would be garages around the back of the apartment block. It was a nicer place than a twenty-year-old should be able to afford on her own; Sadie wondered if her parents were helping her out with rent, or if Rick was himself.

An alleyway went around the back of the apartments. "Cowell, go around the back," Sadie said. "In case he tries to sneak out, if he's here." Cowell nodded and jogged off while Sadie knocked on the door. There was no answer, but hearing movement from within, Sadie knocked again.

A young woman with long, greasy hair and a grubby sweater answered the door. She had a double chin and a slightly piggy nose, but startlingly green eyes with long lashes. Sadie recognized her from the picture on Rick's file.

"Mary-Jane Preston?" Sadie said, trying her best to seem non-threatening, which was never easy when you were carrying a federal badge and a gun, "I'm Special Agent Sadie Price. I need to ask you a few questions."

Mary-Jane glared at her. "About what?"

A few of the neighbors had noticed and were hanging around, trying to listen. The dog was still barking. "Can I come in?" Sadie asked.

Mary-Jane crossed her arms over her ample chest. "No," she said shortly. "What's this about?"

"Rick Tuftner," Sadie said. Mary-Jane flinched, as though she was expecting the statement. Had he already warned her they might be coming to question him? The girl hadn't seemed as surprised as she might have been to have a federal agent at her door.

"What about him?"

"Is he here?"

Mary-Jane didn't answer, just glared down at her feet. "Is he here, Mary-Jane?" Sadie asked again. "Because it's really important that we speak to him."

"No," Mary-Jane said shortly, still glaring at her own feet. Two spots of color appeared on her cheeks. Sadie had no doubt that the girl was lying.

"Mary-Jane," Sadie said softly, lowering her voice, "If you need help to get away from Rick, I can refer you to people who can help." Mary-Jane looked fully at her then, her eyes wide and she suddenly looked very young and very vulnerable. She was about to speak, but then Sadie heard Cowell yelling at her and the moment was gone.

Sadie raced around the back to see Rick running away down the alley and Cowell picking himself up from the floor. "He came over the fence and landed right on me," the state trooper gasped, joining Sadie as they ran after Rick.

"We'll catch him," Sadie said confidently, drawing her gun. Rick hadn't looked particularly fit. Sadie was in shape, and Cowell didn't look like a slouch, either.

"Tuftner! Stop with your hands in the air!" Sadie yelled after Rick. "This is the FBI!"

But Rick carried on running, and as they followed him out of the alley, rapidly gaining on him, Sadie groaned in frustration as she spotted the maintenance van right in front. Unfit as he was, they weren't going to catch Rick before he got into it. Instead, Sadie turned and ran back in the other direction, back to the truck.

"We might be able to cut him off," she gasped to Cowell as she sped back past the apartment and back into the truck. There was no sign of Mary-Jane; the girl had gone back inside and closed the door.

Sadie and Cowell pulled back out onto the main road and then down a small side road, Sadie praying that she had gotten her direction right. She smiled grimly to herself as she saw Rick's van up ahead and hit the gas once more. She didn't think she had ever driven quite so much or so fast in one day. This case was certainly using a lot of gas.

Not to mention energy. Underneath the rushing adrenaline of the chase, she could feel the bone deep exhaustion that she had long been holding at bay threatening to creep up on her, leaving with an almost surreal yet unpleasantly wired feeling, as though she had just downed a quart of the strongest Columbian coffee. She needed, more than anything, a good long sleep and a hot meal. And Sheriff Logan Cooper's arms around her.

Of course, not necessarily in that order.

And not yet. She gripped the wheel, entirely focused now on the van in front of her. Rick was driving too fast, threatening to skid off the still icy road. Unlike the highway, these smaller roads were rarely gritted and were dangerous to drive too fast on. Sadie's truck was built for this weather, but Rick's van, which had seen better days, was not. If he carried on driving the way he was, he would either have an accident, or cause one. As much as she was reluctant to worry about Tuftner's well-being, he was presently a menace to anyone who happened to come the other way.

Not to mention the fact that in her current opinion, a quick death was too good for him, especially if he was the killer.

"He needs to slow the hell down," Cowell said, echoing her thoughts. "He's all over the place."

"I'm going to cut him off," Sadie said, leaning forward and going as fast as she possibly could. Her poor truck was going to take some wear and tear before this was all over.

Cowell stared at her. "Agent Price...I'm not trying to question your driving skills...but..."

"Just hold on," Sadie cut him off as she caught up with the van and started to overtake him. From the corner of her eye she saw Cowell hold on to his seatbelt. She was sure she saw his lips move and guessed he was saying a silent prayer.

"I know what I'm doing," Sadie reassured him. "Besides, I don't think Rick has the stomach for this."

Rick, however, didn't react how she expected him to. Instead of either giving up the chase or attempting to outrun her, he swerved right off the side of the road instead, skidding around so sharply that the back of his van missed the front of Sadie's truck by inches.

"What an idiot!" Cowell yelled as Sadie followed. She wasn't worried; they had him now. If Rick's van wasn't cut out for icy roads, it was even less suited to the snowy wasteland that he was now attempting to drive through. Within minutes the van was stuck in a pile of snow, engine screaming and wheels spinning as Rick tried to correct his error. Sadie hit the brakes, jumping out of her truck as fast as she could wrench off her belt.

Rick had no intention of just sitting there and waiting for them to apprehend him, however. As Sadie reached the van he was already stumbling out of the other side and racing through the snow.

Sadie had to cut across the front of the van to follow him, wasting precious seconds, but Cowell was already there, powering across the snow with his long, galloping gait and tackling Rick expertly from behind, with no need to reach for his gun. As Sadie reached them, Cowell already had Rick Tuftner cuffed, lying on his front in the snow.

"Let him up," Sadie said, her panting breath curling on the frosty air. "He'll freeze to death."

"That would be such a shame," Cowell said sarcastically, hauling the maintenance man to his feet. Rick made no attempt to struggle, but he glared at Sadie from under hooded eyelids.

"Why are you bothering me?" His teeth were chattering. He had run from Mary-Jane's without a coat.

"Get him in the back of the truck," Sadie said, ignoring his question. She watched the man with distaste as Cowell dragged him off, mixed with a touch of grim satisfaction as she thought again of the cruel way the victims' bodies had been displayed.

Whatever part Rick Tuftner had to play in it, she was determined to find out.

CHAPTER TWELVE

Sadie was starting to feel like it was Groundhog Day. Another suspect brought in after resisting, and another local police station that she had never set foot in before. The main interrogation room was in use, and so Sadie and Cowell were crammed into a smaller room about the size of a big cupboard, with Rick Tuftner opposite them. After the way that he had tried to run, he was cuffed to the rickety table leg.

Rick sagged in his chair, looking glum, but there was still a spark of defiance in his eyes when Sadie started talking.

"Why did you move the body, Rick? Not happy with the first place you had settled on leaving her?"

Rick looked blank, then seemed to gather his words together slowly. "What do you mean, settled her?"

"Who was she, Rick?"

Rick looked confused by Sadie's abrupt change of topic, but then he shrugged, a faint sneer coming across his face. "How do I know? Some crack whore by the look of her."

Sadie felt Cowell stiffen next to her and hoped the ex-musician and current state trooper would manage to keep his temper. Cowell reminded her a lot of herself, before a string of high-profile cases and a top-level investigation had forced her to be more mindful of her reactions, knowing that too many eyes were upon her for her to make rookie mistakes due to her impulsiveness, even if it did come from a keen sense of justice.

She couldn't blame Cowell for being angry though; this case was both horrific and had led them on a merry dance all day, driving backwards and forwards across Alaska. Sadie had a sinking feeling they weren't yet done, either; Rick fit the bill in many ways, but now that she was observing him closely, her intuition told her that he wasn't their guy. That he was lying about something, but not about the killing.

Was he covering up for someone? They hadn't yet considered the possibility that the killer could be working with someone; he struck her as the typical serial killer, working alone and in secret, but making too many assumptions could be dangerous.

She should know. The last case where she had made a very big assumption had nearly seen her mauled to death by hungry grizzly bears. That was a lesson that she wouldn't forget in a hurry.

"But you liked the look of her, didn't you, Rick?" Cowell said, speaking through gritted teeth. "You took a shine to her. Do you visit sex workers, or is it just younger women you like alive?"

Rick looked both confused and outraged. "I love Mary-Jane!" His tone was indignant, righteously so, and Sadie would have laughed if it wasn't all so tragic.

"You have a conviction for assaulting her," Sadie pointed out. "That doesn't sound very loving."

"That was just a misunderstanding," Rick said in his best hard-done-by tone. "We both learned from it, and we want to be together. Mary-Jane is a very mature girl. She knows what she wants. She waited for me and got somewhere to live for us as soon as I got out of jail. True love, that is."

"How very romantic," Sadie said sweetly as Cowell snorted in disgust next to her. "She's very different from the woman at the rest stop, isn't she? Did you get bored with Mary-Jane, Rick? Did you just fancy someone different?"

Rick looked down, clearly ashamed, and sensing that she was getting to him, Sadie leaned forward. Maybe Rick really was the killer. She had never seen a man look so guilty, and she had seen plenty of guilty men.

"I love Mary-Jane," he protested, looking at the floor. "I just...need a bit of spice sometimes."

"And killing sex workers provides that spice? What about the Heard sisters? They're more your type, maybe? Did you think Lydia was hot, perhaps?"

Rick raised his eyes to hers, looking both frightened and confused. She had caught him off guard, and the confusion looked real. Unless he was just a darn good actor.

"I don't know any Lydia," he protested. "I genuinely don't know who you're talking about. And I didn't kill that whore. Why are you saying that I did?"

Cowell had heard enough. "Oh, cut the bullshit, Rick," he exploded, his hands balled into fists in his lap. "Why did you run from Mary-Jane's if you're not guilty? Just felt like wasting our time?"

Rick looked as though he was about to cry. "I figured you knew that I …. That I... no. I can't say," he mumbled, looking ashamed again.

"You can't say what? That you moved the body?" Sadie cut in quickly, her voice sharp. Cringing as though he wanted to disappear from their gaze, Rick shook his head.

"Okay, then what is this all about?" Sadie asked impatiently. "Stop playing games with us and spill the truth."

Rick shook his head. "I want a lawyer," he said, sounding more stubborn than he looked.

Sadie sighed. "You're going to need one if you did that," she told him. "Deliberately altering a crime scene is a crime in itself. And unless you can explain what you were doing, you're also looking at a murder charge."

Rick was looking terrified now. "I didn't move her! And I didn't kill her!"

"Where were you last night and early this morning?" Sadie asked.

"With Mary-Jane. She'll tell you that. I started work at seven am." Rick sounded sure of himself now, and Sadie guessed that Mary-Jane would have no qualms providing her much older lover with a false alibi if need be.

"Is one of the rest rooms you maintain the one near Fairbanks?" Quickly calling up a map on her phone, Sadie pointed to the place in question.

Rick shook his head, looking confused again. Sadie was about to question him further on his work schedule when there was a tap at the door, and one of the local police officers motioned for her to come out. Excusing herself, she stepped outside.

"They've got an ID for the victim," the officer outside the door said in a low voice.

"Who is she?" Sadie asked.

"Maria Walker. She's been picked up on prostitution charges, theft and drug, charges plenty of times over the years, including a five-year stretch. Thirty-three, no fixed abode, no next of kin. Seems she was working the rest rooms and shacking up with whatever lonely trucker would have her – or keep her in meth. There was a lot of it in her system. We'll be questioning ex-boyfriends that we know of, but there's no family to notify."

Sadie nodded sadly. Maria couldn't have been more different from the Heard sisters if she had tried, which reinforced her suspicion that the killer was an opportunist, using his ability to come across women at the roadside to his advantage. She had just been in the wrong place at the wrong time, which sounded like it fit with the rest of her tragic life.

"Keep me posted on anything you find out, although given the exact nature of her killing, I would say it's almost certain we're looking at a serial here. Even so, we need to rule out any local connections."

The officer nodded and Sadie turned and went back into the interrogation room. Cowell was swigging a coffee, pointedly ignoring Rick, who was slumped even further down in his chair.

"We have an ID for the victim," she said. She was gratified by the way Rick's eyes flew wide open, guiltily. Cowell looked at her with renewed interest.

"Her name is Maria Walker. Now, tell me the truth, Rick. Did you know Maria? Did you have any dealings with her in the past?"

Cowell looked at Rick, with daggers in his eyes.

"I didn't kill her, or anyone else, honestly," Rick protested. Panicking now, he added, "Look, I did know her. I admit to that. I knew her. I – we had – an occasional relationship."

"Would that have been recent?" Cowell asked.

Rick nodded miserably. "Fairly recent, yes. If you're talking about while I was dating Mary-Jane, then yes. I did know who she was when I saw her, and there were people who – who saw us together in the past. And I realized that – that if anyone had seen us together, and came forward, they might think I'd killed her and that I could be in a heap of trouble. But I didn't do that. And I have no idea why her body was moved. When I saw her, she was in the men's stalls where you found her. I don't know anything more than that. And I want a lawyer."

Sadie nodded. "Sure. We'll get a state attorney down here. You'll have to remain in police custody for now, unless you can provide a firmer alibi. Because you are still a suspect. You did know the victim, you did have a previous relationship with her, you could have killed her to protect your current relationship. Perhaps she threatened you, asked for more money. There are many ways this could have played out, and you could also have been in the right place at the right time to kill the other two victims."

Rick began to sniff in a self-pitying way as Sadie read him his rights. Then the police officer came in to lead Rick to the cells and Sadie turned to Cowell with a sigh, filling him in on the new information. Cowell listened intently but then shook his head.

"But do you think he killed her, though? He has an alibi for this morning. Not that it means much."

"No, I don't," Sadie admitted, "Although the evidence for Maria is stacked against him right now, and he still hasn't accounted for his time, I don't think there's enough of a connection with the other victims. Unless something turns up to link him to the Heard sisters, I don't think he's our guy. And it has to be the same killer given how identical the murders were."

She was starting to think that perhaps moving the body after death was what was important to the killer. Maybe it didn't matter where or how. Maybe this killer was seeking attention, shock value, or to brag that they were a step ahead.

"Well, it won't do that creep any harm to sweat for a while," Cowell shrugged. "So, what now? We go home and wait to see what comes up?"

"Pretty much," Sadie said, then jumped as her phone rang, startling her. It was O'Hara. As soon as she saw his name flash up on the screen, Sadie knew that she wouldn't be heading home just yet.

"Agent O'Hara? Any breakthrough on the Heard sisters?"

"No," O'Hara said, talking quickly. "But you need to get over to the truck stop at Glenallen. A woman was just kidnapped there by a gas tanker driver. Multiple witnesses saw him drag her into the tanker and speed off. Glenallen Police Department are on it, but given these murders..."

"She could be the next victim," Sadie finished for him, feeling her heart pumping in her chest. They could be in time to stop this one from happening. "I'll get right over there."

She couldn't believe these killings were playing out at such a speed. This was beyond anything she'd ever imagined.

She ended the call and looked at Cowell.

"You ready for another drive?" she asked.

Then she sprinted to the car.

CHAPTER THIRTEEN

"He just dragged her into the tanker, right in front of us." The woman blinked up at Sadie, shading her eyes from the late winter sun, now rapidly setting and sending a burnt orange glow over everything. The woman had already told her story to the local PD and the county sheriff but seemed more than happy to relay it once more to Sadie and Cowell.

The Glenallen rest area was a larger one, and two campers full of family members had witnessed the abduction.

"Okay, talk me through what happened," Sadie said, listening carefully for any details that could have been missed. "Where were you when you saw this happen?"

"More or less right here," she said, waving an arm around the forecourt. The small group of people around her included two children bundled up in fur parkas and looking curiously at Sadie, their noses above their scarves bright red from the increasingly biting wind. "The poor girl had just parked up behind our camper there, and the tanker pulled up by the side road about five minutes later."

"And how long had you been here?"

"Ten minutes or so. Just a bathroom break for the kids, you know? We should have been on the road by now," the woman said amiably. Sadie thought that she seemed to be enjoying herself. She wouldn't be surprised if she ended up on the local nightly news. Although Sadie suspected the powers that be were trying to contain the situation to avoid a panic, there had already been a plea for information and witnesses. If this wasn't solved soon, it would hit the press big time, and law enforcement would suffer the inevitable blame for not having done enough, fast enough.

"Can you give me a description of the abducted woman?"

"Sure. She was a pretty girl, and looked quite young, long dark hair, and you could tell she was petite, even under her parka and fur boots. The trucker was a big guy, pale faced, and thick looking, you know? Like a body builder type rather than fat. He was really angry, shouting at her."

"Did you hear what he said?" The woman shook her head and Sadie looked around at the faces of the gathered onlookers. "Did you any of you hear anything?"

One of the kids, a boy of about eight, raised his hand. "He called her a few naughty words," he said. He looked scared, but the other child, who Sadie guessed was his younger sister, giggled at his words.

"And he just pulled her into his truck?" Sadie frowned at Cowell. This didn't sound right.

"Yes. She tried to pull away, but he dragged her. I sent Rachel here to get my husband, but by the time he came out of the bathroom they had already gone."

"I missed the whole thing, or I would have tried to help," the man next to her said gruffly, looking annoyed with himself. "I phoned the cops straight away. We've already told them all this."

The woman who had been talking first peered at her curiously. "Why is it an FBI matter?" she asked, with the air of someone who watched a lot of daytime crime shows. "Has this happened elsewhere?"

"We are investigating related crimes," Sadie said sharply. "For more information, you'll need to contact your local police department and they'll let you know the facts."

She didn't want to cause panic among the local population. There was already information being circulated on the first killings, and a hotline in place, but the police would have the official media statements and would be able to share them. She didn't want to talk out of turn by revealing anything further. Briefly, Sadie wondered if causing a public stir was the reason for the kidnapper's brazen actions. A lot of these killers ended up relishing the notoriety, even to the point of letting themselves be caught.

"And you didn't get the license plate?" she asked.

"It all happened so fast."

"Okay, thank you, you've been very helpful. Can any of you think of anything else that might be useful?"

There was a row of shaking heads. Sadie thanked the crowd again before heading back to her truck. The tanker had gone northward, which led to a fork in the road meaning it could currently be traveling along either the Glenn Highway or the Richardson Highway. The cops had already called for a helicopter and put an APB on every tanker heading that way. State troopers in the area had been dispatched. There was nothing Sadie could do but hit the gas once more and head that way herself.

She wanted to be the one to apprehend this monster. The image of the bodies of the Heard sisters came to her again and she set her jaw as she climbed behind the wheel. Cowell sat down heavily next to her. "All this speeding around is starting to make me feel nauseous," he remarked.

"You're not the only one. But at least we've got a good chance of actually getting this guy now that it's not just us in pursuit." Sadie headed back out onto the highway, her foot flat on the floor of the cab.

"You definitely think it's the same guy? That the kidnapper is the killer?" Cowell sounded doubtful. He was wasted as a state trooper, Sadie thought. He would make a good detective or even federal agent, and she thought his future was bright if he continued in this career. She bet herself that he'd been a brilliant drummer, too, with his focus and passion and attention to detail.

"You're on my wavelength, Cowell," she told him. "It seems way too bold a move. But it's possible –more than possible, I would say, just in terms of circumstantial evidence. A gas tanker, abducting a young woman at a rest stop...what are the odds we have two crazy truckers out here? But it is completely brazen. Maybe he wants to be caught, or he's trying to make sure we notice. Serial killers who go to those lengths to pose, move, and display the bodies are trying to send a message. Some kind of commentary on society or, in this case, what he thinks of women. That's more important to him than not being caught."

"You think he could be one of these incel guys? I keep hearing about them on the news lately." 'Incels' stood for involuntary celibacy, and referred to groups of men, often youngish, poorly adjusted loners, who struggled to find sexual partners and as a result harbored deep resentment towards women and modern society. Forming an online subculture, they were classed as a hate group and had already given rise to terrorist attacks and violence against women, although Sadie hadn't heard of anything quite like this before from a self-declared incel. She could think of other killers who held the same misogynist views though, including the Boston Mangler, the case that had very nearly ended Sadie's career.

"Maybe not officially, but I'm betting he holds similar attitudes," Sadie agreed.

"Well, it lets Rick Tuftner off the hook for sure. He can't be in two places at the same time."

Sadie nodded. In spite of the obvious evidence against him, she felt pretty certain that Tuftner, although flawed in many ways, was no serial killer. He could be released now, and she hoped that his ordeal might force him to rethink his future behavior. At least poor Mary-Jane would have a chance then.

They were approaching the fork in the highway. Sadie was about to ask Cowell to pick a route when another state trooper radioed information through.

"Take the Richardson Highway," Cowell said. Sadie turned the steering wheel and pressed the gas flat down once more. They were traveling at more than a hundred miles per hour and the snowy landscape was whizzing past in a blur of gray. The sun had rapidly gone down and the sky was an eerie purple color.

Sadie kept her eyes peeled ahead, praying the kidnapper would be apprehended before he hurt the woman he had taken. She was horribly aware that if the point of the very public kidnapping was to make some kind of statement, then he would want to kill and display the body quickly before they could catch him. He must know that they were in pursuit after the witnesses at Glenallen.

But how could he know there would be witnesses? It would be a fair assumption, given that it was a busy rest stop at early evening, but something about the whole situation niggled at Sadie. She was missing something about this killer; they all were.

"Do you think the kidnapper could be in league with Rick?" Cowell asked, obviously thinking about events as hard as Sadie was. "Maybe that's why he went off the rails, because he realized Rick had been caught and the game was up."

"I did wonder about Rick working with someone," Sadie agreed. "But given the fact he knew Maria personally, I think it was more a sign of guilt and fear that his dealings with her would be found out."

"He could have been faking that he didn't seem to know about the Heard sisters though," Cowell went on, echoing Sadie's earlier thoughts in the interrogation room. "Do you think he's that good an actor?"

"No, I don't. But I could be wrong. I've been wrong before."

"Not often, so I've heard," Cowell said with an obvious note of admiration in his tone. "You're a hero around these parts. Especially after you busted that trafficking ring at Christmas."

Sadie smiled but felt herself cringe a little inside. A few high-profile cases had seen her end up in the public eye more than she would like. "It was a team effort," she said. "I was working with the Coopers."

"I've met Logan," Cowell said. "He's a good guy. Tough, but fair.

"Yeah," Sadie said, feeling her cheeks go warm. "He is."

Their relationship was so new Sadie wasn't sure if she could even call it that yet, but she had to swallow the uncharacteristic urge to tell Cowell that Logan Cooper was more than a colleague. Sadie had always been an intensely private person, but part of her wanted to shout her and Cooper's liaison from the rooftops. Maybe when all this was over, she would be able to indulge that side of her more.

"Sadie!" Cowell pointed. There was a tanker up ahead. Sadie flashed her lights. To her surprise, the tanker started to slow. Sadie exchanged a look with Cowell.

"It can't be him," Cowell said.

"Let's see." Sadie screeched to a halt, pulling up at the side of the tanker, and jumped out, her hand once more on her gun. She wondered if this time she would need to use it.

"FBI," Sadie barked as she approached the driver's door. "Please step out of your vehicle."

The driver stepped out, and Sadie wasn't sure whether to laugh or groan in frustration.

This wasn't their guy.

"What's this about?" the driver asked as she stepped down from the cab. Her streaky blonde hair was braided off to one side, and delicate features showed this driver was very definitely a woman. She was tall, and had broad shoulders, but otherwise couldn't be less like Sadie's typical vision of an oil tanker driver.

This is why you shouldn't make assumptions, Price, she told herself. As a female Special Agent, she should know better.

"Can I check your license and manifest please ma'am?" Cowell said. The driver reached back into the cab for the documents and Sadie's hand stayed on her gun out of habit. But the woman came back with the required evidence. Cowell flicked through the manifest while Sadie checked the woman's license and radioed through to local PD. She wasn't surprised to find there was no record and no outstanding warrants for the woman, whose name was Joanie Piper.

"Have you seen any other tankers on this road in the past hour or so?" Sadie asked. Joanie shook her head, frowning.

"No, it's been real quiet this trip, actually. What's going on, agent?"

"A girl has been kidnapped by another tanker driver – a male," Sadie told her as she handed the license back. "So if you see anything suspicious, even remotely, call it in straight away."

Joanie looked shocked, her eyes widening, and it occurred to Sadie that with a killer on the loose in the area, Joanie might be as much at risk as any other lone woman traveling the highways.

"You're free to go Joanie," Sadie told her softly. "But be careful. If another driver approaches you for any reason, stay sharp."

Joanie nodded, looking scared as she climbed back into her tanker. Sadie watched her drive off and then went back to her truck, practically stamping with frustration.

"We wasted time there," she said. "We need to get a list of license plates and driver names where possible, or we'll be pulling over the wrong people for days, and the perp will get away."

"I've never met a female tanker driver before," Cowell said. He looked impressed.

They continued northbound, swiftly overtaking Joanie's tanker and driving another ten miles when Cowell's radio went off again and a crackly voice came over the airwaves.

"The suspect has been apprehended outside Paxson and taken to Paxson station," the voice told them.

"And the girl?" Sadie held her breath.

"Alive and well." The radio crackled and went off.

Sadie pulled a U-turn on the deserted road and sped off the way they had come, back towards the side road that led to Paxson, feeling a rush of adrenaline go through her.

"Call Paxson," she said to Cowell. "Tell them no one is to question him until I get there. We're going to find out just what the hell is going on."

CHAPTER FOURTEEN

Sadie couldn't believe this disaster had happened.

"You're telling me," she said through gritted teeth to the police officer in front of her, an overweight guy with a handlebar mustache and a web of red veins on his nose that suggested a drinking problem. "You're telling me that you've released both the suspect and the abducted woman? Together? I asked for them to not be questioned until I got here."

Red Nose sneered at her. "We don't answer to the FBI, Agent Price," he said. Sadie didn't miss the sarcasm in his tone on the 'Agent.'

"This is a federal investigation," Sadie snapped, trying to keep a lid on her temper. These pissing contests between the different branches of law enforcement enraged her. But the cop had no intention of letting it go. His eyes swiveled to Cowell, who Sadie could feel bristling beside her. Cowell was as invested in this case now as she was, and had been just as eager to get to Paxson in the belief that the killer had finally been apprehended and at least one victim saved.

"Why's the trooper here?"

"As the case crosses county lines, we're working together on this. State Trooper Cowell was the first one on the scene of the first crime. His help has been invaluable."

Red Nose shrugged, looking less than impressed. "If you say so."

"Can we cut the BS?" Sadie said abruptly. "Why did you let the suspect go? We've just driven miles at top speed on icy roads to get here to find you've released the current main suspect in a federal investigation. A serial homicide, in fact. So, you had better have good reason, Detective, for releasing a potentially homicidal maniac."

His nostrils flared at Sadie's tone, but the sneer on his face deepened. Whatever it was he knew that she didn't, she realized that he was going to enjoy breaking it to her.

"Your 'suspect' is no such thing. It was a mistake. His name is Tommy Brewster and he's known to us. As is his 'abductee' Amber Harris. Who is, in fact, his girlfriend. They had a fight, and she was refusing to speak to him, so he dragged her into the truck. When we picked them up, they were both most apologetic and Tommy has a solid alibi for the last twenty-four hours; he was in a jail cell after yet another domestic with Amber. Sorry about your wasted time," he finished, sounding not very sorry at all.

Sadie briefly closed her eyes, swallowing her disappointment. She would check all of the facts that Red Nose was telling her, of course, but she knew no matter how belligerent the detective was he wouldn't have released Brewster if he could be in the frame for the killings. She guessed that he was the type of cop who would have loved not just the acclaim of bringing the killer in, but also the chance to do so before a federal agent stepped in.

"But you charged him with kidnapping, right? And referred Amber to the Domestic Violence Unit?"

"No," he said coldly, "because she didn't want to press charges, and because she's as bad as he is. It wasn't the first time those two have pulled a stunt like this, and it won't be the last."

"You don't need her to press charges," Sadie argued. "You have a whole forecourt full of witnesses."

"Yeah, and a tight budget and not enough men," he retorted. "You guys get all the funding. I'm not wasting police time on those two. They left here hand in hand."

Thinking of Rick and his younger girlfriend, Sadie gave a defeated sigh and nodded. As much as it galled her to admit it, Red Nose was right.

Even so," she argued, although her heart was no longer in it, "I needed to question them myself. Or someone could have at least called to let us know there was no point in coming here."

He just shrugged again, and Sadie was too tired to argue her point any longer. She would run a check on Tommy Brewster and his girlfriend, but if he was in the cells at the time of the killings, he was ruled out.

"Well, thank you for your time." Sadie turned and walked out of the Paxson station, pausing on her way to the truck to breathe in the cold air. It was nighttime now, and the sky was clear, the faraway stars twinkling at her, although they brought her no comfort. Sadie had never understood why people liked the stars; they seemed cold to her, and lonely.

"Well, that was a let-down," Cowell said heavily. The strain of the day was showing in his face too and Sadie felt a pang of sympathy for him. As a state trooper, he would hardly be used to working cases like this and they could take a deep psychological toll on those investigating them, as Sadie knew only too well. No matter how many serial homicides she worked, you never got used to it.

"Tell me about it." There was no more to say on the subject.

"So, what's the plan?" Cowell looked anxious, and Sadie stopped walking and looked at him.

"What are you really asking me there, Cowell?" she said. "Do you want to carry on working this with me, or would you rather I bring in another agent? I'm enjoying working with you, but there's no shame in it if the case is getting to you," she said softly.

Cowell shook his head, his mouth a tight line. "I want to stay on it," he said. "Yeah, it's not a barrel of laughs, but after seeing these killings, I'm so angry." He looked at Sadie with haunted eyes, "I need to see him caught."

"So do I. And it's good having you on board, Cowell."

Cowell looked embarrassed and so Sadie turned away and got back into her truck, waiting for Cowell to clamber in the passenger side.

"I'll drop you off at your car," she said, "and then I'll check into a nearby motel. I honestly can't take the thought of any more driving tonight."

"Thanks," Cowell fastened his seatbelt. "Where do we start tomorrow?"

Sadie shook her head. "We need to think about that. We need more leads, because this trail has gone icy cold, and there's not enough evidence now for us to keep holding Rick on the outside chance he was working with an accomplice."

As Sadie revved the engine, she prayed that it wouldn't take another body for them to pick it up again.

*

Sadie sat up in the hard, narrow motel bed with her laptop on her knees. She had run the checks on Tom Brewster and Amber and, as she had expected, there was nothing to link them to the murders and Brewster had indeed been in a cell for the last two days, going straight to find and 'abduct' Amber when he had been released. Nothing had come back from tailing the aunt and uncle of the Heard sisters, although as soon as a second, unrelated body had turned up Sadie had known she wasn't looking at a typical murder, which was often committed by family, friends, or colleagues of the victim, including life partners.

At that thought, she could no longer push away the image of her mother's bones in that mine shaft. It had been only eighteen hours ago, and she had been on the go ever since, chasing a killer and running away from her own demons.

Had it been a friend or family member who had killed her mother? Or killed Jessica?

And then the thought that was always nagging at her that she could hardly bear to think about. Had it been her father?

How else could he possibly know where her mother's bones were? It was surely the only explanation, but it hurt to think about it. Their father had always been a mean bastard, even before the drink took a complete hold of him, but he had loved their mother, and Jessica had been his favorite.

Sadie had never resented her sister for it. Jessica had been everything to her, the one that had protected her from the worst of his drunken rages. With a stab of horror, she wondered if that was why her sister had died – confronting their father about his treatment of Sadie. And then he had snapped.

That still didn't explain her mother, especially when she was dying of cancer anyway. Unless, as Cooper suggested, her father had been trying to put his wife out of her misery.

Try as she might, Sadie couldn't envisage him ever doing anything that compassionate.

She put her laptop aside and lay down, curling on her side. She felt exhausted. Too tired to even call Cooper, she had simply texted him goodnight.

When her phone rang, she knew it would be him.

"Hey, sweetheart," he said, and in spite of her exhaustion and grief the sound of his voice warmed her.

"Oh, it's sweetheart now?" she teased. "I miss the days when you used to just growl 'Price' down the line at me."

Cooper chuckled, then said seriously, "How are you? I'm worried about you. Going straight off on a case after this morning?"

"I'm fine," she said quickly, then sighed and corrected herself. If she and Cooper were going to work as real life partners in a relationship, she had to stop acting as though he was still just a colleague and start opening up a little. "Okay, I'm not fine, but I don't really know how I am. It's been a hell of a day." She filled him in on the case and heard him suck his breath in.

"Sadie, this sounds rough. Can't you ask Golightly to put someone else on it and take compassionate leave? Give that O'Hara a chance to lead up a case maybe." Cooper had met O'Hara on a case she had worked just after New Year, and the two liked each other.

"O'Hara's working on it back at the office, running checks for me, among the other ten million jobs Golightly always has for him. I haven't told Golightly about my mother, and I don't want to. He'll fuss, Cooper, and you know I hate that."

"I know," Cooper said quietly, "But you have to face the fact it may get back to him. It's an open case now Sadie. Currently, it's just me investigating, but I could do with another pair of hands. I was going to pull Jane in, I didn't think you would mind that."

Sadie felt numb. She hadn't yet considered all the ramifications of what finding her mother's body would mean, but of course, it was an open murder case. One that she wouldn't be allowed, as the daughter of the victim, to investigate.

"No," she said, although she felt as though she was speaking through fog, "I trust Jane. I suppose," she said, laughing although she heard the tinge of hysteria in the sound, "you'll have to question me, won't you?"

"We'll need to speak to everyone that knew her," Cooper said softly, the way she had heard him speak before to the bereaved relatives of victims. "So if you remember anything that could be useful...but you know all this. Sadie, can you not consider trying to get off this case? You've been through so much since you got back..." He didn't finish his sentence, but Sadie understood what he meant and felt suddenly defensive.

"Are you worried I'll break? I'm not that fragile, Cooper," she snapped.

"You're the strongest person I've ever met," he said, still in that voice, "but no one is superhuman."

"I can't give up on it yet," Sadie said. "The killer could be on the highway looking for his next victim as we speak."

There was a silence before Cooper spoke again. "Okay," he said, "I'm not going to try and change your mind. Just know I'm here for you, okay?"

"Thank you." Sadie felt tears threatening to spill from her eyes and blinked them away rapidly. "So, do you have any leads on my mother yet?"

Cooper paused again. "There is something I need to ask you about," he said hesitantly, "but I was going to wait until you're back."

"Ask me now," Sadie demanded. "There's no point dragging this out."

"Okay. Do you recognize the name Burt McAfee?"

Sadie felt surprise as the name registered a flood of memories.

"Sure. Everyone knew the McAfee family. They ran the town, in a way. You didn't mess with them. They were powerful and they were dangerous – if you weren't their blood kin, then all bets were off as to how they treated you."

"That so?" Cooper asked.

"Burt had three younger brothers and I think they all died before the age of sixty, in car crashes, fights, and the like. Violent ends. But by then Burt had left town." Sadie frowned, trying to remember what her specific history had been with the family who, instinctively, she'd tried to avoid. But at one stage, she'd seen a lot of Burt. More than she'd wanted to.

"He was friends with my father when I was a kid, although I think they had some kind of falling out later on. I remember I'd try to avoid him when he came visiting. He and my dad seemed to bring out the worst in each other. But I hadn't seen him for a couple of years before I left. He lived up near the Inuit village – his wife was from there."

Her mother's necklace had been engraved with the name the local Inuit had given her for her home nursing and midwifery services. *Mother Dawn*. The same name her father had written on the map he had left her.

That had turned out to lead straight to her body.

Cooper sounded serious. "Burt's wife was your mother's final patient before she got too sick. I went over all the state medical records of your mother's home visits to the village. Do you remember what happened? How Burt and your father fell out?"

"No," Sadie said, confused, although a vague memory nagged at her, of her mother crying. "Did something happen to his wife? I think I can remember Mom crying about it. Didn't she die?"

"Yes," Cooper told her, "in childbirth. Her baby daughter died too. They were caught in a week long blizzard down at the village – there was no way emergency services could get through."

Cooper paused and Sadie knew exactly what he was about to say.

"My mother was her midwife, wasn't she?"

"Yes. Your mother was devastated, apparently. I heard all this from one of the elders at the village. And Burt was devastated, too. He left the village after his wife's death, but the talk there is that he was surprisingly good to her. He treated her like a princess."

"It must have hurt him badly when she died," Sadie said slowly, aware that she was starting to join the dots in her mind, and that she didn't like the picture they were forming.

"Correct. He was devastated. When she died, he blamed your mother, even made a formal complaint. Not that it was her fault," Cooper added hastily. "The hospital was satisfied that she did all she could."

Sadie rubbed her temples, feeling the beginnings of a migraine. "Do you think this is significant?"

"Possibly. It could have just been the grief talking, of course, but -" Cooper paused.

"But what?" Sadie asked impatiently, although a feeling of dread crept over her.

"He had a fight with your dad at the old saloon, just days before your mother went missing. And he was heard screaming that he was going to kill her."

CHAPTER FIFTEEN

Sadie felt stunned by shock, staring around the stark motel room as memories crowded her mind. Finally, she was getting answers – but the answers filled her with a deep dread.

Burt McAfee, a name she'd recalled from long ago. But she'd never dreamed that he would be her mother's killer. And yet, now, it all made sense and she could see it was plausible, and even likely, that he had done this deed.

His threats had forewarned his actions.

Sadie knew how it was out there, in that tough, hard, and remote community. People did take the law into their own hands. Revenge killings were not uncommon, and especially among the McAfees. She remembered whispers of that. Even the cops didn't probe too hard when that family's name came up, and Sadie had always wondered if there was more to that, if the McAfees had gotten the local cops involved in something illegal, and had then used that against them in the future.

At any rate, they had been renegades, who'd done whatever they chose.

In his own grief, beyond reason and without logic, Burt could have taken the life of this innocent woman, so respected by her community. He could have been her mother's killer, and Sadie's chest heaved at the thought. She had never realized that connection before. She'd not realized that Burt McAfee's wife had been her mother's last patient, and one that she'd lost. Now, what had happened made so much sense.

The painful truth was lodged in her mind, impossible to accept, even as she blinked tears of sorrow and regret away.

At any rate, there was no way she was going to be able to get to sleep now, Sadie decided.

She was desperate to find out more about this man, or as she thought of him, this monster.

Sadie decided that right then, propped up against the lumpy pillow, with the flickering motel room light above her, she was going to go hunting. There was no way she could try to sleep. The thought of putting her head down on the pillow, of closing her eyes, was impossible to her. She felt as if she'd identified an adversary and now, she wanted to gain all the information she could on him.

She would find him.

She would track him down.

Would it be possible to accuse him of this crime, so many years later? She had no idea, and feared that the trail might have gone icy cold, and the lack of evidence might make it impossible, but she knew one thing for sure. She was going to try her hardest to make sure that Burt McAfee got the payback he deserved.

She felt the rush of renewed grief and anger, a wave of regret that she'd been too young to protect her mother. "I'm sorry," she whispered, "I'm so sorry."

Logging into the FBI databases, Sadie began multiple searches, looking for information on this man, even as her memory strove to recall more about him.

But she'd been too young back then, and as a young girl in a hard, tough community, Sadie realized now, with hindsight, that she'd automatically sought to protect herself from the people she sensed could do her harm.

The violent people, the heavy drinkers, the ones who fought - just as her father had done - those, she had instinctively tried to avoid. Even at a young age her own self-preservation had been strong, and she'd known intuitively that to survive, she should stay off of the radar of those who exuded destructive rage and violence.

But now it was time to catch up.

While she set searches in motion to scan the state and federal databases, she also turned to the local records, opening up the files that were saved in the small local police department. She knew that there might be limited records, especially going back in time.

Digitization had not come fast to that area, and she guessed that many of the older records might still be paper based, stored away in musty-smelling files on dusty shelves, in the back of the archives room, seldom accessed. She would get to them in time, to see what was there.

But for now, she would find what she could. Serious crimes would surely have made it to the digital database. And if he'd offended in the past twenty or thirty years, she was sure she'd be able to follow the trail online.

Based on what she knew, the man she was looking for had to be in his late fifties now, even his sixties. What could she find out about him?

She worked steadily, her eyes scanning the screen, feeling the rush of adrenaline through her that she was now used to feeling when she was on a hunt.

Burt McAfee was born sixty-five years ago. So he was older than she'd guessed. Reading on, she learned that he had numerous convictions for assault, but Sadie saw that they had all been in the earlier years, before her mother's death. He had a DUI. He'd been involved in bar fights and brawls. The violence was mostly related to drinking, she saw.

But after the date of her mother's death, there had been no further convictions.

She checked the dates twice, looking to make sure, feeling intrigued and confused by what it might mean.

It definitely meant something. She was certain.

Had he finally satisfied his violent urges by killing her? Had that meant he'd no longer felt the need to assault, to fight, to drink heavily?

She doubted it. Sadie pressed her lips together angrily. There was no way that committing a murder would have caused this angry character to reform. No way. He'd shown no signs of wanting to do that in the past, even when imprisoned.

The more likely solution was that after the murder, he hadn't wanted to attract the law's attention to him in case the atrocity he'd committed came to light. And so he'd been more careful after that, and toned down his violent behavior.

She was sure he'd remained the same person. A killer, a cold-blooded murderer, someone who cared nothing for others' lives or well-being. People didn't change, Sadie knew.

Well, sometimes they did, she admitted. Sometimes they could.

But not this time, she was sure of it. This man, this monster, was who he was, and now she saw the rock-solid connection that surely must exist between his own family tragedy and hers.

Fear flared inside her as she considered he could easily have killed Jessica, too. Of course he could have. Perhaps as the years went by, he decided that one life was not enough, and that he needed more.

With a sigh, she admitted the terrible truth to herself. If McAfee had already murdered her mother, then he was set on that path. And in his own twisted mind, she could imagine his logic would dictate that two lives needed to be taken, in exchange for two.

A mother and daughter, in exchange for his own wife and daughter.

The life of the midwife he believed had failed him and caused the death of his family - and in his own terms of rough justice, her daughter, too.

Sadie shivered violently, still feeling cold with shock as this reality hit home.

So, where was he now? What had happened to this man, who'd gone under the radar himself ever since her mother's death? Who'd avoided any subsequent arrests after destroying a family himself?

She learned that Burt McAfee was originally from the east coast, but had chosen to move to Alaska after a hunting accident that left him with a permanent limp. That, now, she thought she remembered. Casting her mind back, Sadie recalled the limp, she recalled the sound of it more than the sight of it, the way those uneven, heavy footsteps on the floorboards had signaled that McAfee was in their home.

She'd always tried to keep away from him, and thus she only remembered the sounds of his arrival, more than the sights themselves.

Just as the rest of his family had done over the years, Sadie guessed that a man like this would have met a violent end, either in a fight, an accident, driving drunk, or even dying by his own hand.

That was a logical conclusion for someone who seemed to spend his life skirting the dark side, wrapped in violence, and living with the knowledge that he'd callously taken lives.

But to her surprise, she could find no record of his death when she went looking. He seemed to be still alive. Living in the hinterlands near her hometown. She couldn't tell exactly where, from the databases. Probably fifty miles out, at least, though. Deep in the wild.

Sadie vividly imagined herself going out there, searching for his cabin, finding him, and forcing him to give her the answers she craved.

Had he murdered Jessica, too? Why had he done what he did?

She bit her lip in anger, so hard that she tasted blood inside her mouth, as she imagined that meeting.

But it was impossible now, she couldn't leave the case she was on. Lives would not be saved by storming his cabin, although her personal quest for answers might be achieved.

Where else could she hunt for him now, in her motel room, while desperately waiting for a new lead or fresh information on this brutal case? Medical records? Would those give any further answers?

She'd just started to search that database when there was an urgent knock at the door.

Sadie had been utterly absorbed, and the sound startled her. She jumped, scrambling out of bed, slamming the lid of her laptop shut as she hurried to the door.

It was Cowell.

His blonde hair looked messy, and his eyes looked tired and red. But he was dressed in his uniform and had pulled on, though not laced up, his boots.

"Sadie, we just got an anonymous tip-off called in," he said, his voice urgent.

Adrenaline surged through her.

"What is it?" she asked. "And where?"

He was already bending down, pulling his laces tight.

"I don't know all the details yet," Cowell said. "But as a result of the tip, a tanker truck has just been found, at the Delta Junction truck stop, with a dead woman in the sleeper cab."

Sadie gasped in a quick breath.

"And the truck driver?" she asked.

"He's in police custody there," Cowell replied, sounding excited.

In police custody? Their killer might be waiting for them already. Now, questioning him and obtaining evidence could be all that was needed to convict this man of the crimes.

"We need to get to the scene, now!" she said, grabbing her bag.

CHAPTER SIXTEEN

Late at night, the usually quiet Delta Junction truck stop was an uncharacteristic hive of activity thanks to this crime. When Sadie pulled up outside, with Cowell in the passenger seat, she saw there were already three police cars parked under the truck stop's bright floodlights that cast glaring beams, and deep shadows, over the stark forecourt and buildings.

She felt a sense of purpose within her, a feeling they had reached the conclusion of this case, and had arrested the perpetrator who had caused such death and destruction.

"I hope this is the killer caught," Cowell muttered, echoing her own thoughts. "I hope we can get this guy, lock him away forever."

But before she could question the perpetrator, Sadie knew she had to take a look at the scene, and prepare herself as best she could by reviewing the evidence. She didn't want to go head to head with this ruthless murderer while being in any way unprepared. She took a moment, breathing in the frigid night air deeply as she prepared herself to take a look at this killer's latest gory work.

"Evening," she said shortly to the nearest police officer as they approached. "Agent Sadie Price. What's the background here?"

The police officer was a short man, wearing a fur hat and a heavy parka. His round face was somewhat protected from the cold by a bushy mustache. He didn't look particularly pleased to see her, but Sadie acknowledged that standing out in the icy cold, late at night, at a bloody crime scene, was not going to make anyone look cheerful.

"I'm State Trooper Jessop, ma'am. We received a call about an hour ago, from someone using a payphone at the rest stop near Matanuska Glacier State Park. They said they'd noticed one of the truckers speaking to a woman on a motorcycle, and that they thought they'd seen him force her toward the tanker truck cab."

"Go on?"

"They were able to give a basic description of the truck. We set off on the hunt immediately, and found it parked up here. When my partner located the driver, Jack Evans, and asked him to open up for us to search, we found the biker's body in the sleeper cab, face up, with a clearly fatal head wound."

"Where was the driver?" Sadie asked.

"He was asleep, in the berthing, in the stop."

Undoubtedly, this was the same modus operandi, Sadie realized. The only difference in the scenes seemed to be where the bodies were dumped, and that didn't seem to be a specific ritual for this killer. Perhaps he'd intended to move her and dump her again, and hadn't yet done so.

"Did he resist arrest?" she asked.

The trooper nodded. "He wasn't too cooperative," he replied. "He was aggressive when we confronted him, but at the same time he swears he's innocent. He said that because he was sleeping in the berthing, in the truck stop building, anyone could have planted the body in his truck."

"So he's using that as his excuse," Sadie said thoughtfully, glancing at Cowell.

Then she turned to the tanker truck, which was surrounded by crime scene tape. She could see that lights had been set up inside, and knew that the medical examiner would be on site, and forensics would already be hard at work taking photos, picking up evidence, as they searched for any clues that might be hidden from the naked eye.

"What about the victim? Who is she?" Sadie dreaded the answer, no matter what name was given. These details were going to turn an anonymous victim into a real person.

"We've identified her as a local woman, Sandy Patterson, aged twenty-four. She has no family locally and was working as a waitress at a diner in Fairbanks. She lives a few miles out of town, and left work at eight pm. It seems she was riding home."

It was time to view the scene. Knowing this would be unpleasant but necessary, Sadie pulled on a pair of latex gloves, climbed under the tape, and stepped up to the cab's open door.

"I'm going to take a look at the body," she told Cowell.

"I'll take a walk around the outside, and see if I can find any prints or trace evidence that hasn't been picked up yet," he replied. Nodding, Sadie climbed inside.

There, under the harsh glow of the police lights, she saw Sandy Patterson's body sprawled, face up, in the constricted space of the sleeper cab.

The wound on her head was identical to the others, and Sadie guessed that the medical examiner would conclude that it, too, had been inflicted by a tire iron. He was working on the body at present, swathed in PPE, hunched over it in the confined space. The cab was cold and cramped, not a pleasant place to work while piecing together the clues from a murder, and Sadie felt a flash of sympathy for the man.

He glanced up at her, his eyes looking tired behind his spectacles.

"This is enough now, enough. I hope we've got the killer in custody at last," he said to her, his voice hard.

Sadie guessed that in life, Sandy Patterson would have been a striking woman. She was wearing tight fitting pants, and her red hair was dyed as crimson as a flame. Her face looked tough and assured, and Sadie had a feeling that she would have been no pushover when alive. A biker girl in Alaska, who stayed alone and out of town, already proved that she was someone who lived life on her terms.

Like Sadie, Sandy had been a survivor. That, she sensed in her. It seemed all the more unfair she'd been robbed of life.

Sadie looked into her dead eyes and hoped she had not suffered before her death.

"Was she killed here? Or was the body moved?" she asked, scooting aside so that the forensic examiner in the truck's cab could have some room to work.

"The body was moved. It was placed inside this sleeper cab after death. Same as the others. That's the only common factor, it seems. They all get moved."

Sadie nodded, pressing her lips together. She didn't like the use of the word 'it' when referring to bodies, but at the same time, she was not going to press that point now, not at the end of such a long, tough day.

Also, the fact she had been moved wasn't the greatest news. A body that had been moved would allow the truck driver to try and wriggle out of the accusations. It would have been much stronger in terms of evidence if she'd been killed while in that sleeper cab.

"Any sign of a struggle?" she asked the ME.

"No, nothing at all. Just the one, deep and well placed blow to the head. Same as the others," he said again. "Same weapon, without a doubt."

Sadie turned to the forensic officer who was searching the cab.

"Is there any evidence you've been able to find?"

"There's a smear of blood that runs from the door to the sleeper cab, and inside, on the seat. That looks to be from the victim, and would probably have happened when she was moved. I don't have anything further yet, but perhaps trace evidence will provide some links," he said.

"Nothing in the truck?" Sadie said, surprised. "No trophies or possessions that could have belonged to the victims, any references to the killing sites, any sign of used gloves or tarps, any evidence of the tire iron?"

He shook his head. "I've been on the lookout for everything you've mentioned, but nothing's come up yet. There's a tire iron in the toolkit that we've bagged up, and also a tarp. They both look clean, but if there's residual blood, it should show up in the analysis."

"Is the vehicle satellite tracked?"

"No. It's an older vehicle, privately owned. No tracking. But there is a manifest, which we've seized and taken into the police department already."

Sadie sighed. It was frustrating to her that right here, right now, they had so little. She hoped the manifest would provide more clues, but a manual manifest could be altered. It wasn't the same level of unequivocal proof that a GPS tracker or a satellite surveillance system would provide.

The less evidence there was, the harder it would be to convict him and the more potential holes in the case there would be. The case needed to be iron-clad. Sadie would accept nothing less.

This killer was so callous, so efficient and ruthless. But, in saying that, she also thought that he was careful. Very careful, and without a doubt, intelligent.

"What about the woman's bike?" she asked, swinging out of the cab and back down to the ground. "Was that left where it was?"

Jessop, the officer who'd greeted Sadie nodded.

"Yes. That bike was where she must have left it, stopped in the forecourt. It looks like she parked and went to use the restroom. My partner tried to start it, in order to impound it as part of the evidence trail, but he couldn't do that. It wouldn't start. He's called out mechanics and they are working on it now, figuring out why."

Sadie raised her eyebrows. This was interesting, and she personally doubted it had been a coincidence. Perhaps the trucker had seen the victim struggling with the bike and had taken advantage while Sandy was stranded.

Or, in a more calculated move, he might even have sabotaged the bike himself, so that he could use the opportunity to walk up and get close to her. Thinking about it, Sadie's money was on the second scenario. She thought that aligned with what she knew of this man. He hadn't escaped police detection so far by being stupid, or by failing to plan ahead. They were dealing with a devious, cunning and intensely violent psychopathic killer.

Now, it was time to drive to the local police department and get face to face with the driver, to see if this man in custody fit this description.

Sadie hoped her questioning could pry the truth from him.

CHAPTER SEVENTEEN

It was after midnight by the time Sadie arrived at the Delta Junction police department, where the tanker truck driver, whose name was Jack Evans, was getting moved from the holding cell where he'd been temporarily imprisoned to the tiny interview room. This was it - the make or break questioning that would decide, or deny, his guilt.

And while trace evidence might be scarce, at least the physical evidence of the victim's body in his truck provided a good start.

Pulling up outside, she shivered as she climbed out. This wasn't just late night chill. She sensed that the temperature was dropping sharply. A biting wind was gusting from the north, and clouds looked to be moving in.

"We got some weather coming," Cowell said, pulling his jacket tighter as he observed the sky. "Looks like a snowstorm, or maybe an ice storm, blowing in. By this time tomorrow, I'll guess the whole area will be shut down."

"I hope by then we've closed this case," Sadie said.

"Me, too," Cowell agreed, as they headed into the police department. There, a state trooper, who was a woman and looked to be in her mid-twenties with thick, brown hair and deep blue eyes, was waiting for them. Her badge said 'Merrow.'

State Trooper Merrow's blue eyes looked tired, Sadie thought, as if it had been a long working day for her, too. But she greeted them efficiently, and offered coffee while the suspect was transferred to the interview room, which Sadie accepted gratefully.

"Does Jack Evans have a record?" she asked Cowell in a low voice, as they clustered into the back office, hastily gulping down the brew.

"Let me check," he said.

He checked the case documentation, and then moved toward one of the old-looking computers in the office, quickly tapping keys as he logged in.

"Evans is clean. No speeding tickets, no hit and run, no offenses involving drinking and driving. He has never been in trouble with the law before. Never been questioned in connection with any type of crime. Even his driving record is clear, and he's had no accidents." Cowell sounded disappointed, the same way Sadie felt.

Although she'd been prepared for the fact that this killer had kept under the radar in the past, a criminal record would provide another layer of proof. She wanted this case wrapped up tight. If Jack was their man, then there was no way Sadie wanted him getting off on a technicality, or managing to convince the jury he'd been an unlucky victim of circumstance. Not on her watch, she thought.

She wanted him locked up forever.

With Evans's background providing nothing further to add to the case, they headed through to the interview room at the back of the building where their suspect had now been moved.

At least it was warm, Sadie thought, walking ahead of Cowell into the environment where the small window was tightly closed, and the rattling heater issued a stream of hot, dry air.

Staring across the desk, she took her first look at the suspect that she hoped was the criminal they had been hunting.

Evans, who was fifty-one years old according to the records she'd glanced at, looked a couple of years older in real life. His hands were cuffed together, the sleeves rolled back to display darkly tattooed arms.

The fact he was cuffed meant he'd caused trouble when arrested, Sadie knew. The tattoos didn't raise alarm bells for her. At a glance she could see no gang insignia among this ink, no other signs or emblems to indicate potential trouble.

Ink alone meant nothing, and Sadie knew you'd have to look far to find a trucker without it. She recalled that even the female trucker they'd briefly questioned earlier in the day, had some artfully done tattoos on her arms.

Rather, it was Evans's face and his expression, that was making her feel they were on the right track here.

His face was as hard as nails, with a bulky jaw, tight lips, and narrow, dark eyes. He had a scar on his right cheek, a pale slash in otherwise weathered skin. Undoubtedly he would have been strong enough to wield the tire iron, which in any case, would have taken only 'average strength,' she remembered.

His face was expressionless, but his eyes were unblinking, his gaze unfaltering. He was challenging her, she thought, staring right back at him. He was breathing rapidly.

"I'm Special Agent Sadie Price, FBI, and we need to question you regarding a series of murders, Mr. Evans," she said, introducing herself as she sat down and checked the recording equipment was working.

"State Trooper Cowell," Cowell introduced himself. He pulled out a small notebook and jotted something down.

"So," Evans said, sounding deceptively casual, "you guys are going to frame me for this, are you? Is this what you do? You're incompetent and can't research a case properly, so you just look for someone to blame?"

Sadie remained calm. If anything, she was pleased that Jack was looking to fling insults and accusations. It meant he had a loose mouth on him, and that gave them a better chance of success in getting him to spill out something in a temper.

Something such as - vital evidence, a hint that could be construed as a confession, or even a motive, announced in anger.

Something valuable that would let them walk out with a solid conviction.

Yes, she far preferred people with a temper. She hoped that Evans would become more intense as their talk progressed.

She could see that the less experienced Cowell, however, was rising to the insults and looking affronted by Jack's words.

"You don't have any evidence," Evans went on. "Not a shred."

"There was a dead body in your truck, Mr. Evans," Sadie pointed out.

Evans's eyes turned feral. "What was in my truck, I had no hand in. You can't blame me."

"Someone saw you struggling with her and called it in on the crime hotline. They said you were forcing her into your truck. Then she's discovered in the sleeper cab? I think a jury would take that as fairly strong evidence. Don't you? Did you murder her, and then throw her into that cab?"

Evans looked incredulous, and then shook his head.

"Whoever said that, is lying. I didn't fight with anyone. I didn't force anyone into my vehicle. I've never seen this woman before. Some psycho dumped her there. I might not have locked my truck up. Who locks up, out here in the sticks? We're all in this together, or so I thought. Nobody is gonna steal anyone else's gear in the middle of nowhere, on a freezing night. "You think I'm some dumb trucker, right? You're thinking I'm stupid, aren't you? I turned in early. I was tired. I was asleep when you barged in and dragged me out of my berth."

The man spoke calmly, but with a simmering rage behind his words, Sadie thought.

"Let's have a look at your manifest," she said, opening the folder she'd brought in with her that provided a basic record of his trips. She wanted to do this in front of him, to see his reaction as she paged through it.

"I'm looking through this so that I can track your movements, based on the series of killings along this route," she told him, watching him carefully.

But there was nothing. His expression didn't change, she noted.

But as Sadie did a basic check, she also noted that, unsurprisingly, his route had taken him along the exact area that the killer had used. Apart from one small deviation, and a few discrepancies in timing, but the paper form in that area was blurred, as if he'd spilled something on it.

Maybe in an effort to cover up that it had been erased, Sadie thought.

"Not going to find anything there," Evans spat. "I want to see my lawyer."

Sadie noticed that Cowell glanced at her and then looked away, as if he wasn't sure whether he should argue with Evans.

"We'll allow you to make a call," Sadie said. "As soon as I've checked this."

Evans shrugged. "Suit yourself. You won't find anything. You guys are incompetent."

"You don't even know us!" Cowell protested, rising to the bait. "We're the ones who have to clean up the messes that murderers leave behind! So are you saying you're one of them? Are you the killer? Because I'll tell you what I noticed. You never showed a shred of sympathy!"

"I was shocked, of course!" Evans shot back. "As for sympathy, I never even knew her. I never saw her before this evening, when they took me along to my own truck. She sure as hell wasn't there on the way to Delta Junction. You think I wouldn't have noticed a corpse in my own truck? How stupid are you?"

Cowell let out an angry breath, and Sadie decided it would be better to take over the questioning before this escalated into a verbal war. She didn't want Cowell to compromise the questioning through his own hot-headed desire for fairness.

"Is it right you didn't see anything?" Sadie asked, glancing at Cowell. "You're not hiding anything from us? Can you prove you checked that area?"

He looked edgy. "I'm not hiding anything. Not a thing. I'm not guilty."

"Did you make a stop at the rest stop near Montuska Glacier State Park?"

"Yeah, I did. I refueled there."

So the tip-off had been correct, Sadie thought. And the fuel log showed he had stopped, even though there was not any evidence that he'd stopped at the earlier stop near Fairbanks, where the Heard sisters had been found. But that could have been an unscheduled detour.

"Why is this manifest damaged here? Did you try to erase something, or want to cover up your changes?"

"No. I keep good records. It got damaged there. By coffee. I spilled my coffee when I was working on it. That was just before I went in to the berthing to get some rest. So you go ahead, if spilled coffee is what it takes for you to lock me up unfairly then be my guest. It's what I'd expect from you. You guys, you're all corrupt. If I had money I'd buy you off, but I don't, so yeah, you got a good one here. It's a coffee stain. Coffee. That's as wild as I got, in my truck, before I turned in."

He pointed, awkwardly because of the cuffs.

She saw Cowell tense, and his eyes narrow. For a moment, Sadie wondered if he was about to retaliate angrily to the accusations of corruption.

But then, she saw what Cowell had noticed.

It made her hesitate, too.

He'd pointed with his left hand.

Was he left-handed? She felt a flare of concern that a small but highly relevant detail like this could end up derailing the case completely. Without a doubt, the medical examiner had found that these murders had been committed by the perpetrator, using their right hand.

Not only had the blows been hard, but also accurate. Yes, people could be ambidextrous, but this was going to be an unwanted issue that might end up weakening the case.

And most definitely, if he lawyered up, a good lawyer would instantly argue that this meant the killings were impossible.

It was time to check.

Sadie glanced at Cowell.

She stood up, walked around the desk, and undid his handcuffs.

"Am I free to go?" He gave her a nasty smile, evil in its confidence. "Have you decided to bully someone else?"

"No. We're only just getting started here. But first, I want you to sign your name on this page for me," she told him, placing the handcuffs on the shelf. With both herself and Cowell in the room, she didn't think he'd try anything.

"Here," Cowell said, raising the pen he'd been using. "Catch."

He tossed it across the desk to Evans, while Sadie watched intently to see how he would catch it.

When Evans caught the pen expertly in his right hand, Sadie let out a breath of relief.

Angrily, he stared at her, before lowering his head with a frown to sign his name, and she noted that he did this, too, with his right hand.

Undoubtedly he was right-handed, and they'd confirmed this as a team without even letting him know what they were doing.

Evans then massaged his left bicep with his right hand, kneading the shoulder as if it felt stiff or sore. Watching him, Sadie was now wondering if he'd pulled a muscle or strained something – perhaps when moving the body.

"The manifest shows you were at the sites where the victims were taken," Sadie confirmed. "Give or take a few minor detours."

"Why don't you have GPS tracking in the truck?" Cowell asked.

"Why should I?" Evans replied argumentatively. "It's my truck. I know where I'm going. I keep a manifest of my stops. That's all the taxman needs from me. I know the area and I don't see a need to waste money on any additional tracking." He sounded angry and defiant. But Sadie saw he was sweating now. Perspiration was rolling down his face, in fact.

"Did you know the victims? Did you speak to Sandy before you picked her up?" Sadie pressured. He really was not looking comfortable, she saw. Not at all. He was shifting in his chair. His shoulders were hunching.

"I don't know what you are talking about," he said. "You guys, you must let me go. Just leave me alone."

Sadie stared at him, eyes narrowed. There was something going on here, she could see, and she didn't like it. Not at all. She didn't like what this meant. It filled her with fear.

"Mr. Evans," she said, in a voice so different from the one that she'd been using that Cowell turned to her in astonishment. "Do you feel okay? Physically, I mean? Are you on anything? Do you take any medication? Have you taken any substances?" she asked, urgently now, as the man was starting to sway in his chair.

"I take nothing. Nothing. But I - I don't feel so good," he said.

He was sheet white, she saw. Blue-white. He was gasping for breath.

Leaping out of his own chair, Cowell caught Jack just before he collapsed.

CHAPTER EIGHTEEN

"He's having a heart attack, I think," Sadie gasped, staring in consternation at her suspect, who was now slumped on the desk in the interview room. He would have been slumped on the floor if Cowell hadn't been grasping his shoulders. She literally couldn't believe this. Somewhere between the stress of the questioning, the lateness of the hour, and this man's physiology, a tipping point had been reached.

Now, they were not just fighting to get answers, they were fighting to keep him alive.

"Get the ambulance!" Sadie shouted, bursting out of the interview room and rushing through to the front office. "Our suspect has collapsed. He needs a hospital, urgently."

The state trooper was already on the phone, her face intent.

"It's on its way," she said, a minute later.

Sadie rushed back to the interview room, where Cowell had loosened the man's tight belt, removed his jacket, and was checking his pulse.

"I can't - I'm finding it - difficult to breathe," Evans muttered. He was panting for air. The man's face was clammy, and his breathing was thin and shallow.

"Keep talking to him," Sadie said to Cowell. "Keep him conscious, if you can."

She rushed outside to wait for the ambulance, almost gasping as the freezing wind hit her. It was even colder now, and the contrast between inside and outside was dizzying.

She felt totally conflicted as she waited.

They hadn't gotten any kind of a confession from this man as yet. He'd denied and denied. But what if their own questioning had caused this to happen? What if the pressure of the interrogation had resulted in this man breaking down and suffering a fatal health challenge?

Sadie didn't want anyone wrongly accused, and nor did she want to have an innocent man's death on her hands.

But equally, they had no other suspect. There was only Evans. He was the one who fit the description, the parameters they had put in place. He'd been at the crime scenes at the approximate times.

Even so, she couldn't shake the guilt that if she had pressed ahead unfairly, then it might be her fault that this man was lying slumped in the interview room, gasping desperately for breath, as if his life was slipping through his fingers.

She rushed back to the lobby, staring anxiously out into the cold night, and to her relief, she heard the scream of approaching sirens.

With a flash of lights, the ambulance arrived. Two paramedics climbed out and rushed in, carrying a stretcher and a haversack filled with equipment, and Sadie led them through to the interview room, hoping they would be in time.

Then, she left the interview room, getting out of the way so that they could work in the confined space.

Returning to the police department's postage stamp sized lobby, she waited anxiously with Cowell until she heard the rattle of the stretcher wheels approaching.

"He's stabilized for the meanwhile. We're taking him to the hospital now. We've called ahead to Fairbanks Memorial Hospital and let them know he's coming in."

"Thanks," Sadie said.

As the paramedics left, she turned to Cowell.

" Evans is still a suspect," she explained. "Can you organize a police guard at the hospital? I'm sure they won't allow police in ICU itself, and I'm certain that's where he's headed, but there needs to be a guard as close by as the hospital allows. We'll need updates on his condition, and to be given the heads-up when he's cleared to be questioned again."

This delay was all the more frustrating because of the looming storm. If there ended up being an area-wide shutdown, they needed to be close to him, and ready to jump in again as soon as possible.

Cowell nodded, looking determined. "I'm going to make a few calls now, and get the police guard organized," he said.

While Cowell did that, Sadie headed back to the interview room. She picked up the pen that Evans had used, got the notes together, and packed up the manifest. With the room straightened out, she returned to the lobby, feeling stressed in a whole lot of different directions.

Nothing about this day, and particularly tonight, had gone the way she'd thought it would. She felt as if there had been shocks and bombshells waiting at every turn. Despite their best efforts, they had not been able to prevent a fourth victim from losing her life, in the killer's third strike. And as yet, Sadie had no conclusive proof to present to her own bosses.

Circumstances beyond her control had ensured the current debacle.

Feeling discouraged, she climbed into the car with Cowell.

"We need to find a hotel in Fairbanks, as close to the hospital as we can get. If Evans is stabilized by tomorrow, we need to be on site to continue the questioning, and I'm worried about this storm."

Cowell nodded. "Yes, I think we'd better head into town. There's a hotel near the hospital, according to my maps app. We could even get a few hours of sleep." He sounded hopeful.

Cowell seemed surprisingly cheerful, so much so that Sadie felt reluctantly admiring of her partner's resiliency.

"You know, one of the things that the boys in the band always used to say is that everything happens for a reason," he said, as Sadie started the car and got on the road, speeding toward Fairbanks.

She glanced dubiously at him. Glad as she was that he was taking this in good spirits, she wasn't in the mood for accommodating any tired philosophical platitudes. Her fuse was way too short for that.

"For a reason?" she snapped out tersely. "I don't believe that."

"It's true," Cowell said, blithely unaware of the fact her mood was worsening as rapidly as the weather. "You see, by tomorrow, forensics could have found some actual evidence in that truck. Some real proof that Evans will have difficulty denying. That'll put us in a much better situation."

"True," she said reluctantly.

"Or else, he could just feel ready to talk about it. Especially if he's survived a heart attack, spent time in ICU. It might change his mind. He might be more ready to open up to us."

"I can see you're trying hard to convince me," Sadie grumbled, but she did feel slightly better to her surprise, as the lights of Fairbanks came into view, the city swathed under a blanket of deepening cloud.

"It's all we can do. And to be honest, I can use the shuteye now," Cowell admitted. "Questioning him with a fresh mind might help."

"That's also a good point," Sadie admitted with a sigh.

But as they headed toward the three-story, modern hotel where a few welcome hours of sleep awaited, she found her anxieties flaring all over again. An unwanted thought loomed in her mind, impossible to budge.

If this man was not their killer - if he was innocent of these crimes - then it meant someone else was out there.

And this delay in the investigation, together with the worsening weather, meant that the elements were on the killer's side, and not on hers.

What if tomorrow morning brought the news of yet another death?

CHAPTER NINETEEN

Sadie awoke with a jolt, the pealing sound of her phone tearing her out of a surprisingly deep sleep.

She fumbled for the phone, nearly knocking it off the bedside table in her haste to pick up the call. This bed, in a small but well equipped room on the hotel's third floor, had been far more comfortable than the board-like one at the motel. Although her sleep had been filled with malevolent dreams, she had at least rested well.

But she'd still been dreading what news the morning would bring.

It was Cowell calling. She grabbed it up.

"Hi," she said rapidly. "Any updates?"

"I've had some news from the hospital," he said. "The police on duty there got a report and called me straight away."

Sadie planted her feet on the carpet and stood up, ready to take in whatever bombshell landed.

"What did they say?" she asked, already moving to the cupboard where she'd hung up her spare shirt, ready for the morning.

" Evans is out of ICU and in high care. It wasn't a heart attack, apparently."

"What was it then?" she asked.

"A lung embolism, on the left side of the chest. Doctors said that if he hadn't gotten to the hospital as quickly as he had, he would probably not have made it. Luckily they were able to diagnose it and dissolve it, while he was on oxygen. He didn't need a ventilator, but it was touch and go."

"So if he hadn't been sitting in that interview room with us...?" Sadie asked.

"Yes, if he'd been in the truck stop berthing, it might have been a worse prognosis for him. Same if he was on the road. Even more likely he wouldn't have made it."

Sadie blinked, feeling surprised and relieved that the reason their main suspect was still alive, was that he'd been getting interrogated at the time. At least she didn't have to shoulder the guilt that she'd nearly killed him. Whether or not he was their killer, that wasn't something she wanted to have to live with. But the embolism would have happened regardless. Being with the police had saved him.

"When can we question him?"

"The doctor has to do his rounds, but it looks as if we might be able to speak to him later this morning," Cowell said. "He's much better. Apparently he's complaining about the food, and saying he wants to get out of there."

"Don't let him run," Sadie warned, anxiety flaring inside her. A man who was feeling well enough to run, would be a real flight risk, especially if he had secrets to hide.

"There's a police guard stationed outside the ward," Cowell said. "And if we head there now, we can wait outside, too."

"Let's head there straight away," Sadie agreed. "Meet you downstairs in twenty minutes?"

She cut the call, realizing that since they had to await the doctor's clearance, there was no huge urgency to get to the hospital. Therefore, she might as well have a shower. She'd been too tired last night, and had fallen straight into bed.

Sadie rushed to the bathroom and turned on the faucet as hot as it would go, which proved to be very pleasingly close to a boiling point.

Sadie got in and stood under the steaming needles of water, knowing without a doubt that this was the warmest she would feel all day, with this ice storm on the way.

Being in the shower, relaxing as it was, gave her a few minutes to think, to take in everything that had happened yesterday. It gave her the chance to wonder, yet again, if there was something she'd overlooked.

The evidence couldn't point to Evans more strongly. Without a doubt, the body in his tanker truck was incriminating.

But why would he have left a body in his truck, while turning in to get some rest at the stop? Why not dump it somewhere? Although there was no pattern to what had happened after the kills, there was a common thread in that all the bodies had been dumped, and swiftly.

What if this one had been dumped, and the truck was the dumping ground? What if she was just a little bit wrong in her thinking, and needed to perceive things from a different angle?

She remembered again how it had felt, that moment when Evans had pointed with his left hand instead of using his right.

How she'd immediately feared that they were wrong.

She'd been able to test that theory, but what if they were making other mistakes, other wrong assumptions?

They'd thought that Evans was having a heart attack. That was what it had looked like. But that had been wrong, because it had been a pulmonary blood clot. Still serious and potentially fatal, but not what they had thought.

So what else were they incorrectly assuming in this case?

Why was she having doubts about Evans as a suspect, despite his uncooperative attitude? The truth was, she acknowledged, a lack of cooperation didn't automatically make someone guilty. Everyone had their own baggage, their own past experiences, and many people didn't trust law enforcement here, particularly individualists.

The problem with an assumption was that it was hard to know you were making it, because it became entrenched in your thought process.

She remembered Cowell's cheerful words, trotting out the tedious reminder that everything happens for a reason.

But sometimes, Sadie knew, you needed to grasp the situation in both hands and make your own reasons.

She dried her hair, changed into fresh clothes, packed up her bag and rushed downstairs, meeting Cowell in the lobby on the stroke of the twenty minute deadline.

"Are we heading straight to the hospital?" he asked. "I mentioned that Evans might be a flight risk and they've got two cops outside now, not just one."

"No," Sadie said.

"Why?" Cowell looked surprised.

"I want to spend a few minutes reviewing the case notes first. And while we do that, let's call forensics and find out if there's any update on any trace evidence, at all, in the cab of that tanker truck. We can head into the café here while we work."

She was determined to make the very best use of this extra time they had.

While Cowell made the calls to forensics, Sadie gathered up her case notes, reading and rereading them, looking for the inconsistencies they might have missed, the loopholes they maybe hadn't seen. Surely if they looked hard enough there would be something to find?

What were they missing? What wrong assumptions were they making, that might mean they were focusing too hard on an innocent man, and not seeing the evidence that was waiting there, if they looked?

Cowell got off the phone with a disappointed sigh.

"They've been over the vehicle with a fine-tooth comb," he said. "There's nothing. Nothing at all that indicates any of the victims were kept there."

"Nothing?"

"Not a trace of blood, not even on the tire iron. All there is on it is old oil. There's also nothing in the truck that could be used to transport a body without leaving a trace. You know, plastic wrap, tarps, coverings, that sort of thing?"

Sadie sighed. "Yes, I do know. And the absence of all of that is going to count against us heavily here. Because those victims were transported, for sure. Whether dead or alive at the time they were moved, it would be difficult not to leave any traces of them, even if they were wrapped up. One, you might get away with. But four?"

Cowell nodded agreement. "What does this mean, then? Have we missed something? I don't see how we could have, but what if we did? I mean, I've been over the little details again and again and I can't see that we've slipped up anywhere."

"Me neither," Sadie said, feeling totally discouraged now. This case was imploding around them. The lack of trace evidence was a huge blow. She'd been so sure, deep inside, that something would be found.

"Maybe it's not a little detail, but something really obvious, like - hiding in plain sight?"

Something about Cowell's words matched up with Sadie's own thoughts, with what she'd been thinking earlier, that they'd made a wrong assumption.

And then, with a chill, she realized there was a detail.

Goosebumps prickled her skin as she thought about this possibility. It had to be worth exploring.

"There's one very important fact I need to confirm," she said, and hearing the tone of her voice, Cowell sat up straight, looking enthused.

"What's that?"

"The anonymous tip-off that was called in yesterday."

"What about it?" Cowell now sounded mystified, but there wasn't time for Sadie to explain further.

"I need to speak to the officer who took that call. Urgently."

CHAPTER TWENTY

Sadie could see Cowell was curious and confused, not understanding why she needed to follow up on the tip-off. But now that she'd had the theory, it was rock solid in her mind. It made sense. It was suddenly like seeing daylight, understanding at last how this might have been done.

But it all hinged on a detail that she needed to confirm.

"I'll get hold of Jessop," Cowell said.

Sadie glanced out of the window, noticing that the wind was getting up. The roadside trees were swaying violently in the gusts. With the sun not yet up and the sky blanketed by clouds, the early morning view looked gray and foreboding.

And yet, Sadie was so focused on her theory that she barely noticed the grimness of the weather.

The waitress refilled their coffee cups, while Cowell made the call.

"It's Cowell here. Is Jessop in yet?" He paused, grimaced impatiently. "Okay, if he's not in, that's fine, but I need to know a detail. It's about the caller who sent in the anonymous tip about the woman being abducted."

Sadie watched anxiously as Cowell nodded.

"You can get it? That's great. That will be first prize for sure. Can you call me back on my cell?" He waited again. "No, I don't know why. My partner, Agent Price, requested it. She has a theory and thinks it might be important. Good. Thanks."

Cutting the call, he turned to her.

"We got a lucky break here. Because this case is so serious, Jessop put a policy in place that all tip-offs were recorded, so that they didn't miss a detail. But he wanted to remind you that the voice note is all they have. The caller remained anonymous and the number didn't have caller ID."

Sadie felt a flare of excitement. Finally, and none too soon, it looked as if they were getting a break in this emotionally wrenching case.

"That's fine. They're getting the recording?"

"They are. They're going to call it up, and then Jessop's partner, who I spoke to now, will call me back on my cell. They're looking for it right away. They should call back any moment."

He paused. Gulped down some coffee.

Sadie wondered if this meant there was light at the end of the tunnel at last, that it didn't feel as if they were blindly stumbling into darkness. If the recording confirmed what she thought, then it was a game changer in terms of the case.

She needed this case to be over, this killer caught, for justice to be served at last.

Sadie felt done with trying to hold back her own pain. The emotional toll of what she'd learned about her mother and her sister, and about McAfee, felt as if it was about to burst its walls. She was trying to contain it, but whenever she lost focus or her will faltered, emotions flooded in.

Now, as she waited, her thoughts strayed to Cooper, and she wondered what he was doing now on this cold, early morning. And that gave Sadie a flicker of comfort. Thinking of him, his strength, his ability to retain a calm mental balance in the face of adversity, helped her feel that it was possible for her, too.

She could do it, for just a little longer.

And then Cowell's phone rang. He grabbed it off the table.

"Cowell speaking. Yes, great. We'll listen together, just a sec. I must put this on speaker."

Thumbing the phone quickly to speaker, he placed it on the table between them, looking at it expectantly.

Sadie stared at it too, finally allowing herself to feel excited about her theory. The next few moments would tell her if it was right or wrong.

"Okay, here goes," the man's voice said. "I'm putting it on now. I'll play it through, and then you can let me know if you want it replayed."

"Copy that," Cowell said.

There was a pause and a crackle, and then a tinny voice sounded.

"I'd like to report something unusual I just saw," the speaker said.

Sadie sat bolt upright. She drew in a quick breath. Already, she could tell this theory was correct. She was right. At this critical time, she was right.

The recording continued.

"What do you want to report, ma'am?" the officer taking the call asked.

"It's at the truck stop near Matanuska Glacier State Park. I saw something happen there a short while ago, and when I talked to my friend about it, she said there was a hotline I could use because it might be connected to these murders. I've just seen -"

Sadie drew in a breath, this time of excitement and triumph.

"Thanks," she said. "You can cut the call. I've heard enough."

Now, Cowell stared at her as if she was crazy.

"But - but the actual eyewitness report hasn't even begun yet."

"It doesn't matter. I've heard what I need to. Thanks," she called, for the benefit of the helpful officer in the police department who'd called back.

Cowell stabbed the disconnect button.

"So, what is important about this call?" he asked.

"It's a woman speaking," Sadie said.

Cowell's brow furrowed. "And why's that going to help us? I'm really confused. How does that make a difference?"

Not only was the voice unmistakably female, but in spite of the poor quality voice recording, Sadie thought she recognized it. There was something about the intonation, the accent, that struck a chord in her memory.

"We pulled a driver over yesterday. A woman," Sadie said. "She was driving a tanker truck. Name of Joanie Piper."

"You think that's her?" Cowell frowned. "But you can't really tell from the recording. Why do you think it's important? Do you think she could have called in this warning? You think she knows the killer?"

"I think she is the killer," Sadie said firmly, and Cowell's arm jolted in surprise, sending a splash of coffee onto the table.

"Her? A woman?" he asked incredulously. "But we - we've been looking for a man, all this time."

"We have," Sadie agreed grimly. "And we've been wrong, Cowell. We've allowed our own preconceptions to influence us, by thinking that only a man could have done this. But the coroner said it would have taken average strength. A strong woman could easily have made the kills. And more importantly, from what I remember, that truck manifest backs up my theory."

"What about it?"

"I took a look at it yesterday, and I remember that truck was traveling via every place that a kill has been made. Matanuska Glacier State Park, Fairbanks, and Wasilla. All the names on that list were familiar. She's been at every affected site."

How she wished she'd realized this earlier. This woman had been the killer. The victims had trusted her, most likely. Allowed her to get close. They hadn't seen the danger. And Sadie had been so focused on her preconception that it was a man, it had taken her far too long to realize the truth – that it was a strong, female killer.

Now, she couldn't unsee it. All the pieces were falling into place.

"Hell!" Cowell uttered. "But couldn't that be coincidence? It seems like such a stretch, to think a woman did this. And she seemed so innocent. I mean, she pulled over for us immediately. She helped us." He shook his head, clearly wrestling with this idea.

"Looks deceive," Sadie insisted. She knew that only too well. Whether male or female, a psychopathic killer often had an uncanny ability to blend into society as well as an ice-cold nerve, something that Cowell clearly hadn't experienced.

"I'm still not sure," he admitted. "I mean, how would she have done that?"

"She could have killed Sandy Patterson and put her in her own truck. Then she followed Evans out on the road, waited until he pulled over for the night, dumped the body in his truck, and then - only then - made the anonymous call to say she'd seen something."

She could see Cowell's mind speeding ahead as he thought over every shocking twist in this case, the facts they'd been wrong about, that now they were relooking at, made sense. She felt oddly calm, as if this was the way it was supposed to be. The pieces of the puzzle had fallen into place at last.

"I'm still finding it hard to believe, but yes, I can see it's possible," he said. "I guess it's the only thing that makes sense. But we didn't suspect her, not for a moment. In fact, if I recall, we warned her to be careful. And she seemed so – so normal. So calm." He looked astounded that they'd been so focused on the fact that a man had been preying on these women. "We didn't even take any of her details. We just checked them, and let her go. Now, what are we going to do? We don't even know her vehicle's license plate."

"We can still follow the trail," Sadie insisted, and a moment later, Cowell also joined the dots for himself.

"We need to get to Delta Junction, and now."

"Let's get on the road," Sadie agreed. "We've got a serial killer to catch."

CHAPTER TWENTY ONE

There was no time for 'if onlys,' Sadie knew, as she and Cowell raced out of Fairbanks, heading at speed for Delta Junction. But she couldn't help regretting that she hadn't worked this out earlier.

Now, they were a few critical steps behind in this chase, and there was every chance that Joanie Piper was not only far ahead, but also ready to kill again.

They needed to catch her before that happened, Sadie resolved, gripping the wheel as she wove through the morning traffic, speeding out of town. But there was still so much they didn't know.

Sadie's truck didn't have a dashcam, and that was going to count against them now, when every moment was important. If they'd been in a state trooper's car, with a dashcam as standard equipment, then they could already have called in the number plate of the tanker truck they'd stopped yesterday, with Joanie Piper on board.

As it was, they were now playing catch-up, needing to find her vehicle, and check if she'd been caught on camera at Delta Junction. That would give them an idea how long she'd stayed there, and that in turn would help them calculate where she might be now.

"I'm going to look her up meanwhile. Get some background checks done," Cowell said. Sadie could hear from his voice that he still felt doubtful. He wasn't as sure as she was.

Sadie didn't have time to do anything but focus on her driving. But she was aware that Cowell was on the phone, talking fast, gathering information on their newest and strongest suspect.

If only, Sadie thought. If only they'd looked into her more closely, if only she'd had the flash of insight yesterday that the killer did not have to be a man. They'd had her! They'd literally been face to face with her and they'd let her go!

Sadie swerved out to pass a slow moving truck, timing it so close that the oncoming car flashed its lights and honked its horn.

"Have some patience, why don't you?" Sadie growled under her breath. "We've got a criminal to catch."

Shooting back into her own lane just in time, she turned on her own emergency lights, not wanting to activate the siren while Cowell was trying to get the all important information over the phone.

As she remembered the conversation they'd had, she was worried by how calm the woman had appeared. No wonder Cowell was finding it hard to accept. Joanie had been icy cold. Nothing in her voice or her demeanor had clued Sadie that she was even remotely worried about being stopped by two law enforcement officers who were hunting - for her.

She'd pulled over so obediently. Compared to the other renegades they'd been chasing down, that had felt like a big surprise. Immediately, Sadie had assumed the driver had nothing to hide. That thought had been so instinctive.

That scene had been cunningly and coolly handled.

And there would have been a wealth of trace evidence in that tanker truck, Sadie was sure. If only they'd taken their search just one step further and had a look. The case could be closed by now. She thought back, trying to remember any details as they got onto the highway, speeding toward Delta Junction.

Nope, no details were coming to her. She remembered it was a standard silver truck, not brand new, not ancient either. Entirely ordinary in every way. No branding on it that she recalled.

But now, speeding into Delta Junction truck stop, she hoped that despite its ordinary appearance, they could get some footage of the truck arriving. There weren't that many tanker trucks on the road yesterday, and they had a clear idea of the window of time in which she would have had to arrive to dump the body.

Cowell got off the phone as Sadie parked hurriedly.

"Okay. I've got background. She's a freelance trucker by occupation. Doesn't work for any one company so it might be her own vehicle, or belong to a private company. And no police record."

"What about her address?"

"They're getting her home address, but that database is down, so it'll be a few minutes. Maybe longer. I've just got one more call to make."

"I'll take a look at the footage," Sadie said. "That, at least, we can do now." She glanced around, glad to see that there were visible cameras in place. Since this was a rest stop with berthing and amenities, she guessed it was an essential security precaution.

They rushed to the truck stop's offices, which were nothing more than two squat, basic, converted containers. The other buildings, beyond, didn't look much fancier.

Walking into the office, Sadie breathed in the smell of old, damp carpeting that flavored the musty, warm air.

A tired looking woman with yellowing blonde hair and visible, outgrown, dark roots, glanced up at her from behind the tiny desk.

"Help you?" she asked. In no way did her tone sound even remotely helpful.

"FBI Agent Price," Sadie introduced herself quickly. "I'm looking for footage from yesterday evening, in connection with the local murders," Sadie explained.

The blonde tightened her lips. "I'm not authorized to do that. I need my manager's permission. The police were here the whole of last night just about, asking questions. Shouldn't you have looked at the footage then?" she retorted, in a tone that told Sadie exactly what she thought of life in general, and law enforcement in particular. Most probably, she'd had to work late last night. Now, she was tired and grumpy and sick of the whole situation.

But Sadie seriously did not have time to waste. Irritation flared inside her that they were coming up against this level of obstruction at this crucial time.

"We have new information now," Sadie asked, ignoring the 'I'm not authorized' line and struggling to stay polite. "This is a public safety issue. I really need to see this footage."

"I know these murders are serious. But my boss had to delay this meeting because of all this yesterday. He told me he wasn't allowed to be interrupted, so all I'm saying is you'll need to wait for him to be available," the blonde insisted, in a tone that caused Sadie's blood pressure to spike. "He is very worried about all of this, of course. He's worried people won't use the truck stop anymore after this happened, and also that our insurance premiums might end up being raised. So we're feeling like we're at the end of the rope with all this police interference. That we might end up getting blamed for it when it wasn't our fault at all."

"This is an emergency," Sadie hissed, but she could see that the blonde's lips were pressing together, and she was folding her arms across her ample chest.

"I'm going to need to get authorization on it, ma'am. I don't want to be in trouble for showing footage without my manager's okay. We're in enough trouble already."

"Then call him!" Sadie threatened.

"As I've said, he told me this morning he's in an important meeting."

Sadie took a deep breath, feeling her self-control crack, ready to unleash eight levels of hell on this uncooperative assistant. Nine, in fact, if that's what it would take.

And then, Cowell walked in and hearing the door clatter, they both looked around. The blonde looked at him with a completely different expression.

"Hey, Bronwen," Cowell said, hurrying to the counter. Sadie felt surprised, and then realized that of course, having spent time in the nearby area and playing in a band when he was younger, Cowell would most likely know many people in town.

Within a moment, the woman's entire demeanor had changed. Her arms unfolded. A winsome smile warmed her face. Sadie thought, to her astonishment, that she even did her best to flutter her eyelashes.

"Hey, Cowell!" she replied. "How's the policing going? Are you still doing your music part-time?"

"Yeah, now and then. On weekends, I sometimes help out if there's a band that needs drums or guitar."

"Do you have any lined up?"

"I might be playing at Tony's Eatery this Saturday. I've got the weekend off. Assuming we're able to solve this case," he added. "Otherwise I'll still be at work. I heard you say you can't show us the tapes, but I really need your help. This footage could help us catch a killer."

"Really?" she said, as if this was news to her, as if Sadie herself hadn't told her exactly the same thing.

"Yes. We've got new information we need to check. It's nothing that will get you in trouble at all. It's just making sure if the killer stopped here, and identifying the vehicle. Then we'll be on our way, chasing it down."

"Okay." Sounding positively cheerful to be of help, Bronwen produced a key from the drawer and unlocked a door leading into the cubicle-sized back office.

Feeling thankful that Cowell's intervention had oiled the wheels, Sadie crowded inside with the others.

"Here's the timeframe we need. From seven pm through to nine pm," Cowell said.

Now in a much more cooperative mindset, the attendant called up the footage and scrolled back through it to the starting point, before playing it forward in fast motion. Sadie watched intently, noting every vehicle, keeping her eyes peeled for the moment they needed.

She saw nothing suspicious, just a steady stream of trucks, cars, and campers.

Until suddenly, there was Evans's rig pulling in.

Now, the hunt was on because Joanie would have been following closely.

The minutes flicked by. And then, there it was, a silver tanker truck, approaching the rest area.

"That's it!" Sadie let out a triumphant breath. Now she recognized it, and so did Cowell, who was nodding confirmation. He noted the number plate. The truck drove directly through the forecourt, heading for the rest area parking beyond. That was where Evans's tanker had been waiting. But if Joanie had dumped a body, it had been done out of view of the cameras.

"I'm going to make a call and check up quickly," Cowell said, hurrying outside.

How long had Joanie stayed there, Sadie wondered.

"Can you keep going?" she asked the attendant, watching the footage flick past.

The police cars came and went and then returned. She saw forensics and the coroner arriving. There was her own truck, caught on camera. There, at last, was Evans's truck, being driven out to the vehicle pound after being searched.

And then the hours went by, late into the night and early into the morning. To her surprise, Sadie realized this woman must have overnighted here.

Ice cold! With all the police around? That seriously took some nerve, she thought.

Only at five am, just a couple of hours ago, did she finally see the silver tanker truck come into view again as it left. Was it really her? Suddenly Sadie doubted herself and wondered if she'd been wrong. She needed to double check with Cowell.

"Thanks," Sadie said to the attendant, who glowered at her, defaulting to her 'unfriendly' setting once more.

As she swung out of the small office, she met Cowell coming back inside. He was holding his phone and looked excited.

"It is her truck. Registered in her name," he said.

"That's great," Sadie said. It meant that Joanie was out on the road now. But not too far ahead.

"And also, I've gotten her home address," Cowell said triumphantly. "She lives close by. In Tanacross."

Sadie nodded, the plan of action solidifying in her mind. That might mean she would lay low until the police activity had died down. And that meant that there might be trace evidence in her vehicle that she didn't want picked up if there were any stop and searches in the area.

"Let's get an APB out on that tanker truck now. And then, we go to Tanacross, in case she's driven home."

CHAPTER TWENTY TWO

The drive to Tanacross should have taken an hour and a half, but with her lights flashing and siren blaring, accelerating as fast as she dared, Sadie made it in a little more than an hour. She knew that every moment mattered in this chase.

The weather was closing in. Clouds were starting to loom, forming weird, threatening shapes as if whipped by the wind. She was hoping that with the storm now seriously threatening, Joanie would have decided to go home. With her own tanker truck, her livelihood, to look after, it would be the most sensible decision. Especially since Sadie hoped she still considered herself to be free and clear. After the innocent encounter yesterday, Joanie surely could not believe the police would suspect her.

Tanacross was a tiny town, Sadie saw. The temperature there felt frigid, as if the cold was actually starting to attack them as they drove into the surprisingly scenic town, with a scattering of snow-covered homes, backed by a dark border of woodlands and then, far away, framed by a range of icy white mountain peaks.

They pulled up outside the small, low, single-story home where Joanie resided, at the end of the town's second side street.

Sadie climbed out, the icy air catching in her lungs. Clouds thronged over, invading fast, swallowing up the snowcapped mountains even as she watched. The cold felt like a solid force.

"This is one of the coldest places in Alaska, I believe," Cowell said, pulling on his gloves as he got out. "Strange that a killer would hole up in such a tiny, peaceful place."

He still sounded doubtful, but Sadie wondered if perhaps Joanie enjoyed the isolation. Maybe the starkness appealed to her.

She wondered briefly, looking at this small home, what had happened to turn her into a killer. Why had she snapped? Why had she gone on this homicidal spree?

Wherever the answers lay, one thing was for sure, their luck had run out again for now.

"It doesn't look like she's home." Sadie could hear the tone of her own voice, flat and disappointed. Joanie hadn't been home for a while, clearly. The snow outside was undisturbed. No sign of a tanker, and the small garage was closed.

But perhaps someone was home.

"Let's check."

Cowell knocked on the door. They waited. No answer.

Sadie was growing impatient. It felt like her own internal clock was ticking faster by the second, so great was her sense of urgency.

She knocked, harder this time. No reply.

"Do we enter and take a look?" Cowell asked.

Sadie hesitated. "I don't think we have enough probable cause to search without a warrant," she said reluctantly. Even though she was burning with curiosity to know if there were any clues in Joanie's home, she had to admit that the chain of evidence, so far, was fragile. And Joanie was a cunning, intelligent woman who could easily have kept all traces of her misdoings out of her home environment.

"We could see if a door is open? Maybe she didn't lock up?"

Sadie sighed. "No. We can't do it. It would end up compromising the case. We can apply for a search warrant. That's all we can do. We could organize that now. In the warmth," she added, because this wind was cutting with all the force of daggers.

Feeling frustrated that Joanie hadn't done the logical thing and driven home ahead of the storm, Sadie hurried back to the car, feeling chilled to the bone even after that short time outside.

And then, as she reached for her phone, ready to call Golightly and ask him to organize it, fast, the radio in her car crackled to life.

"We've got a hit on the APB," an officer radioed through. "The vehicle in question arrived at the truck scale in Tok about fifteen minutes ago. Footage just came through from the highway camera."

Sadie caught her breath, seeing her own excitement in Cowell's eyes.

Tok was just down the road, a little more than ten miles from Tanacross.

Suddenly, the trail was no longer cold.

Sadie started up the car and they roared away, heading for the weighbridge, knowing that wherever Joanie was now, she had to be close. Close enough to be within their reach at last.

*

When Sadie arrived at the truck scale, she saw the place was empty. There were no trucks currently in the area. Jumping out, she rushed over to the office.

Inside, a blast of heat greeted her and a bearded man looked up, surprised, from reading a magazine.

"FBI," Sadie introduced herself. "You had a truck pass through a little while ago?" She showed the man the number plate details. "We're pursuing this vehicle. Anything you can tell us will be helpful."

"Yes, that's right." He checked on his list and looked up a computer record. "This vehicle was headed southeast, toward Tetlin Junction." He paused, and tapped more keys. "And according to its weight, it's currently empty."

Empty? So Joanie was not on a delivery. Was she picking up? If so from where? But Sadie was starting to fear that she was choosing this route, with an empty truck, for a different reason. She might be trying to reach the Canadian border, and if she did, then it would vastly complicate this case.

Sadie's heart was racing now. She was running on pure adrenaline.

"Can we make it to Tetlin Junction in time?" she muttered to Cowell.

She didn't know the answer. But she had to try.

"It's only a few miles away," Cowell said.

"We need to get on the road, then, and fast," Sadie said through gritted teeth, as they burst out of the office and sprinted back to her car. "We need to get more personnel on this chase. Can you get a helicopter out?"

As soon as they were in the car, Cowell got on the radio, doing just that as Sadie sped along the highway to Tetlin Junction. But the news wasn't good. The crackling exchange told Sadie that a helicopter was not possible. Not now, with the weather closing in. It was too dangerous for them to fly.

"Any other backup?" she asked desperately.

Cowell shrugged, looking as frustrated as she felt. "I've requested it. But out here, right now, we might be on our own, because it doesn't sound like anyone else is close by."

They were on their own. And the ice storm was starting. Whirling, sharp flakes of sleet were sheeting down, closing in their visibility to no more than a few yards ahead. Narrowing her eyes, turning the wipers up to max, Sadie peered through the maelstrom, driving as fast as she dared, aware of how slippery the road had suddenly become.

Her mind was working furiously, thinking over all the possible scenarios, the different ways the situation could play out and the consequences that might follow if she and Cowell were not successful in catching up with Joanie.

Tetlin Junction was just a couple of miles ahead but it was nothing more than a fork where two highways met, and a lonely looking gas station with a tiny store and restrooms was located on the side.

But not so lonely, Sadie saw, with visibility clearing slightly as they approached. Not so lonely.

There were a couple of trucks parked at the gas pumps.

And one parked further on, near the side of the road, just before the gas station's exit.

"It's the one," Cowell said, pointing. "That's her vehicle! The plate matches. Now we've got her."

Sadie pulled up behind the tanker truck in a screech of brakes, and jumped out, her hand on her gun.

CHAPTER TWENTY THREE

Sadie gripped her gun as she and Cowell stormed up to the silver tanker truck. Finally, they had caught up with Joanie Piper's vehicle. Would she be inside?

Sadie rushed to the driver's door.

"Cowell, cover the back," she said, looking for movement. She didn't trust this not to be a trap. This woman was a killer and highly dangerous.

She hammered on the driver's door. "Joanie Piper. FBI. Open the door."

There was no answer from inside the cab. Sadie stepped up, grabbing the handle, looking inside the tanker truck's partially misted window.

She drew in a sharp breath.

There, on the passenger seat, she could see a dark stain that looked suspiciously like blood. The keys were in the ignition. A crumpled tarp was on the floor in the passenger well.

With more than enough cause now to search and enter, thanks to this visible evidence, Sadie wrenched the door open.

She recoiled as she breathed in the distinct whiff of dried blood emanating from the tarp. With a flash, she remembered how Joanie had gotten out of the truck to approach them when they'd pulled her over. No wonder she'd done that. It had been skillfully done, and had stopped them looking inside.

There were rubber gloves, several pairs, some discarded, some bloody. A pink scarf, bundled up behind the seat, and a woman's wallet. Sadie pulled on a glove herself, and opened the wallet.

She drew in a quick, sharp breath as she saw it belonged to Sandy Patterson. There was her ID card and her driver's license.

There was more than enough proof, in this truck, to convict the driver.

Sadie reached in and tugged the keys out of the ignition. She had no idea where Joanie was, but she didn't want her driving away right now.

And thanks to the ice storm shutting things down, they surely had a chance of finding her. In fact, Sadie was sure she knew where Joanie must be. She was in the truck stop building, either using the restroom, or buying some supplies at the kiosk.

"There's enough evidence in here," she shouted to Cowell, clambering down. "We need forensics here, and fast. But now, we need her, and she must be inside!"

Sadie pointed to the buildings.

Guns drawn, they raced there, getting a startled glance from a tall trucker with a heavy beard, swathed in a parka, who was leaving.

They burst in.

The restroom entrance was inside the main building, which was little more than a shop selling the basics.

A heater was rattling behind the counter, but there was nobody in attendance at the kiosk. As they watched, another man headed out of the restrooms and walked out of the building.

"The restrooms. She has to be there. I'll search the women's, you take the men's?"

Sadie stormed down the short corridor and wrenched open the door. To her surprise, though, there were only two stalls in the tiny space, both empty. She wasn't here.

Feeling disappointed, Sadie hurried back to the kiosk, and a moment later, Cowell returned.

"She's not inside," he said.

"Where the hell is she? Did she hitch a ride? Climb into someone's truck?" Sadie asked, feeling confused and desperate. She could not believe that this woman was still managing to stay ahead this way. How was it even possible?

At that moment, the entrance door banged open, and the bearded man who'd just walked out rushed back in, with panic on his face.

"My truck's been stolen!" he announced breathlessly. "It's disappeared. I was only in here for ten minutes, and it's gone! My phone's in there!"

He looked at Cowell expectantly, clearly identifying his state trooper uniform.

"I went to the restroom and then came back and waited for Louise to ring my stuff up. Eventually I gave up on that and went out, to find it gone. I need it! It's got valuables inside! This happened now!" His voice was rising.

"We'll handle it immediately, sir," Cowell said. While his voice stayed calm, he looked at Sadie in a panic. She felt the same way he looked. Without a doubt, their fleeing fugitive had opportunistically taken this man's vehicle. But that wasn't what worried her the most.

What worried her the most was the missing store attendant. With all the restrooms empty, Louise was not behind that counter.

With a clench of pure fear, Sadie realized that Joanie was on the run again - but she was not alone.

She must have captured another victim.

She grabbed Cowell's arm and pulled him away, speaking in a quiet voice, so as to be out of earshot of the desperate trucker.

"She's taken Louise, I think," she said, quietly. "And we have to find her."

"I've got my whole life in that rig! I need it back!" the truck owner implored.

"Okay," Sadie said. Now that she'd appraised Cowell of the situation she found herself strangely calm, the icy control of her training and experience overriding her need to scream and wave her arms in despair.

"Please, give us a description, sir. And the plate details."

Sadie saw that in the commotion, a tow truck had stopped outside and the driver had walked in, and was listening with interest as the trucker shouted, "It's a driver's rig, towing a flatbed with a yellow backhoe. I was delivering it across the border."

"We'll find it. We're going to get on the road now," Sadie said, still in a calm voice.

But Cowell grasped her arm. "I'm worried. Look here, see the map?" He pointed to the road map on the wall behind the kiosk. "This highway splits. If she's heading south, she could choose two different directions. The south branch is the Alaska Highway, the north branch goes up to the Top of the World Highway. She could have taken either one of them," Connor explained.

Sadie pressed her lips together as she considered their new dilemma. They now only had a fifty-fifty chance of choosing the correct road. Both led to Canada. Both were less than fifty miles from the border.

They needed to split up, and they needed two vehicles. Using the killer's truck was not a viable option. Preserving the evidence inside it was critical to the murder case. And that meant they needed to ask a favor from a stranger instead.

She hoped sincerely that at this time, they might possibly get the help they needed, instead of coming up against yet another person who hated the police.

Summoning all her charm and composure, which at that stage felt sorely lacking, Sadie turned to the tow truck driver who'd just walked in.

Trying for a nice smile, she said, "We're hunting down a suspected murderer who we believe has just stolen this man's rig. We desperately need to outflank this criminal. Could we borrow your tow truck, so that one of us could use it? That way, we can search both branches of the highway."

The tow truck driver's eyes widened. This was clearly akin to asking if Sadie could have his first-born. But the trucker stepped in, with an impassioned plea.

"Please, brother, help a man out here. I've got cash in that cab. My phone's there! My life's there!"

Sadie could see the tow truck driver's mind working. Clearly he was astounded at the idea that a couple of cops had driven up, and in the space of a few minutes, had so totally lost a criminal that they needed to borrow a ride to help them. This was clearly not a normal day.

Luckily, a moment later, he relented.

"Sure," he said, handing over the keys to Cowell, who accepted them in his outstretched hand. "Just be careful with it, okay? The weather's closing in. I mean, things could get bad. I was planning on waiting the storm out here."

"I will be careful," Cowell promised.

There was no time to lose. Sadie was already hurrying out of the kiosk.

"You take the south branch, I'll stick to the north one," she said to Cowell. "Stay in touch by phone. Call if you see her and I'll be there, fast."

Then there was no more time for planning. Rushing out into the buffeting wind, with flying snow stinging her face, Sadie ran for her truck.

CHAPTER TWENTY FOUR

Conditions were worsening fast, Sadie saw, feeling tense as she hit the gas, speeding along the north branch of the highway as fast as she dared. Which was becoming slower and slower, despite all her willpower and all the skill she was using.

The snow was coming down in icy, blinding torrents, and the blacktop was barely visible. Every so often, she'd feel a stomach-lurching bump as she veered off the road and onto the snowy hard-pack flanking it.

Quickly, Sadie corrected herself yet again, biting her lip in tension. It was pretty much insane to be on the road right now, still less chasing down a killer.

But the thought of the kidnapped victim drove her on. There was a possibility that Louise, the innocent store attendant, was still alive. In the rush to steal a new ride and get her victim out of the store, Joanie might not have had time to make the kill. That was what was keeping Sadie going, even though her sense of safety and logic were screaming at her to stop, that this pursuit was inherently unsafe, and could result in the loss of three lives, instead of only one.

But she knew that if there was a chance of saving that one life, then it was worth the risk - to her, at any rate.

At that moment, her phone rang.

It was Cowell on the line.

"I'm here on the Alaskan Highway," he said. Signal was terrible. His voice was fading, breaking up into static, and then clearing for a moment. She felt her stomach clench that he might have found Joanie. If he had, how would she get to him in time?

"What's happening?" she asked.

"There's been a crash. A gas tanker coming west just lost control and ended up rolling. The driver's gotten out, luckily, but there's gas all over the road and it's now on fire. It's blocking the road completely."

"So you can't get past?"

"Not a chance. I've got the driver in this tow truck. He's bruised and banged up some."

"His safety comes first," Sadie admitted. No way could Cowell abandon his sworn duties as a state trooper. He would need to take the driver back to a safe place, to ride out the storm and hopefully then get medical attention.

"Yes, that's my thought, too. The problem is that if the crash occurred after she passed, then she's free and clear. She got away. I can't get past this crash site. No way. Not till it's cleared."

Sadie closed her eyes briefly and then opened them in a hurry, not daring to lose focus on the road ahead for a moment.

"There's no way of getting past that crash, so you've done what you can," she said, her voice hard. "Take the driver back, and get help in Tok. And return the tow truck to its owner. I'm sure he'll be glad to see it in one piece."

"Will do," Cowell confirmed.

Although the northerly route was the riskier one with the storm closing in - which was why she'd opted to go that way - the southern route would have made more logical sense for Joanie to follow. Bracing herself for disappointment, Sadie acknowledged they could well have lost her completely. This could mean the end of the road for now, and a massive delay in the investigation, if she crossed over to Canada. They might never find her. In the Yukon wilderness, it would be all too easy for a fugitive to hide.

And then, just as she was considering abandoning the hunt, believing that nobody could possibly be pushing forward along this road in this weather, Sadie saw a dark shape looming ahead.

She hit the brakes, her truck sliding and slithering on the ice, as she recognized the shape of the flatbed with the large, looming, yellow shape of the backhoe atop it, up ahead.

She was here! She must have pulled over, trying to escape this lethal weather, just as any sensible person would do.

But then another, darker, thought occurred to Sadie. The question was - had Joanie pulled over just to get out of the storm, or had she stopped in order to kill her victim, knowing the snowy conditions would provide the perfect cover for dumping the body?

Sadie pulled open the door and gasped out loud as the cold hit her. The ice storm was back in full force, with the snow coming down even more thickly than before. But it was the gusts of wind that were making these conditions particularly brutal

Heart in her mouth, she scrambled out of the truck, almost landing on her back as she slid on the ice, and rushed up to the flatbed, grabbing onto it so that she could stay on her feet.

And that was all it was, Sadie saw, shock jolting through her as she realized what had happened. Just the flatbed. No cab attached.

Realizing that this heavy weight on the back of the rig was slowing her down and probably causing the entire rig to slide dangerously, Joanie had simply uncoupled the entire thing and left it where it was.

Was there any sign of the hostage she'd taken? Had this been a reason for abandoning the load - to leave the body there?

Heart in her mouth, Sadie clambered up onto the flatbed and peered into the backhoe's windows.

Nothing. There was nothing there, no trace of a body, and from what she could see in the rapidly frosting windows, no trace of blood or a weapon either.

That meant the killer, and the hostage, were still on the road, plowing inexorably northeast in these murderous conditions.

Shuddering with cold after the few minutes spent out of the car, Sadie returned to it, her legs and feet feeling numb with cold, her feet clumsy on the pedals and her hands almost unable to feel the wheel.

Cranking the heater and windscreen demister to the max, she forged onward, knowing this was crazy, a foolish mission, but needing to try.

Needing to save one life, if one life could still be saved.

But as she battled the ice storm, Sadie knew she couldn't keep going much longer. Her truck had less grip than the rig's powerful cab. The tires were slithering around on the ice and visibility was now so poor that she was effectively blind.

In a whirling world of white, she had no idea at all where the road was. It was dizzy, disorienting, and it was the enemy of speed.

She was crawling along, adrenaline spiking, the speedometer stubbornly stuck at 10 miles an hour, because she could go no faster, not without risk of driving off the road completely. This felt hopeless, an impossible endeavor. She didn't know how she was going to go on.

Perhaps it was time to hit the brakes, try to turn, and call it a day.

Another gust of wind almost knocked the car sideways. She was driving blind, now, unable to see anything because the sleet was covering her windscreen again, faster than the wipers and the comparatively fragile heater could remove it. She was still freezing after being outside for just a minute in these conditions, her body numb with cold, her hands clumsy. For her own survival she should stop, now.

But Sadie shook her head. It didn't matter how many times she told herself that was the best thing to do.

It wasn't. No matter how terrifying this ride, it was nothing compared to the terror the hostage must feel in the stolen rig - assuming she was even still alive.

And nothing compared to the terror that other victims would feel if Joanie got away, because one thing was for certain, she was on a murder rampage and most likely, incapable of stopping until she was caught. Many more innocent women might die at her hands.

She had no idea how she was going to keep on, but she had to. It was now a matter of refusing to give in, of continuing to push forward, even if she was risking her life in the process.

Gritting her teeth, Sadie pushed on at her frustrating crawl, feeling the car getting physically battered, slewed sideways by surges of wind blasting from the north.

And then, she saw it. In front of her. Two faint but discernible tracks.

The marks of tires in the snow.

Her eyes widened. She'd managed to make headway. She'd caught up enough that she was following the tracks, and now, they were guidelines in the snow that would allow her to move faster.

Hitting the gas, flinching as the wheels spun, Sadie eased the car to a higher speed.

Focusing on the tire tracks as if they were her only lifeline, and praying that a snow gust wouldn't obliterate them, she continued.

And in another long minute, coming into view a few yards ahead of her, she saw a dark shape loom and knew with a flare of triumph that she'd done it.

She'd caught up with Joanie's stolen ride. And now, she had to catch her.

CHAPTER TWENTY FIVE

She was gaining ground. Minute by icy minute, in the buffeting storm, Sadie was creeping closer to her target. Joanie was ahead, and in these conditions, she couldn't simply drive away and outpace her hunter. Both of them were trapped in weather so severe it was beyond what Sadie had ever imagined.

This slow, inexorable pursuit was unlike anything she'd ever had to do before. Risking more speed, Sadie eased her truck faster to try and narrow the gap. Her hands were tight on the wheel. It would only take a moment's loss of focus to lose this chase. She could so easily become mired in the huge snowdrifts that were now piling up on each side of the tracks.

The heavy, high riding cab ahead was literally forging a path through the snow that Sadie had to follow, or lose. And if she lost, there was everything at stake.

She kept her eyes on the frustratingly vague shape, obscured by flying snow, watching as the cab fishtailed on the ice, sliding far too much for Sadie's liking. The snow was flying constantly, a blizzard of flakes that had to be blinding the driver. That would work to Sadie's advantage, surely? Because in these conditions, it was easier to follow behind, than to find the road ahead.

But as Sadie got closer, she realized she must not make the mistake of underestimating her adversary.

Brakes flashed ahead, as the cab suddenly slowed. Sadie gasped, wrenching at the wheel. This was entirely deliberate, she realized. Joanie had done this on purpose in order to try and cause Sadie to crash. And as her truck slewed on the ice, Sadie realized that her plan was about to work.

The brakes were nonfunctional on the packed ice, and now her truck was careening forward, on a collision course with Joanie. Even a small rear end impact might damage the engine. It would be enough to strand her, while probably leaving the rear of the tall, heavy and solid cab undamaged. And being stranded now, without a working engine, would mean certain death. She'd watch while Joanie and her hostage drove away, and then it would be too late.

"Come on, come on," Sadie muttered to her truck, her teeth gritted, her hands welded to the wheel.

She could see the cab ahead. She was going to hit it. She was helpless to stop the collision.

Eyes wide, she cranked the wheel in a last, final effort. It slid, then held. Slid again, and veered sideways, now on a collision course to sideswipe the cab.

Swearing, Sadie wrestled with her wheel, fighting the skid, trying to pull her truck away onto the far side of the road.

She got traction for just a moment, and was able to veer sideways, avoiding the rear-end collision she'd dreaded.

But on the ice, she still couldn't stop. She'd veered, but she couldn't stop. And, to her horror, she found herself passing Joanie's cab. Now she was in front, still fighting for control as her vehicle swerved and spun. It was a downhill, Sadie realized, her heart accelerating. In this flying snow and crawling along at a snail's pace, she had not understood that they were on a steep downward section of the highway and this was now the reason why her truck had turned into a runaway.

And as the cab loomed in her rearview mirror, she realized that Joanie had seen her lack of control and she was going to use it. Joanie was going to use the only weapon she had readily available - the big, solid cab itself - and she was going to try and run Sadie off the road.

She couldn't go faster. On the downward slope, she was already out of control. Joanie had far more control in her weather-appropriate cab, with its powerful engine and big, rugged tires.

Sadie hit the brakes again to no avail.

The cab knocked against the back of her truck and she gasped, grabbing the wheel as she was jolted completely off course. The truck spun, careening on the road, and in the white-out, Sadie had no idea where she was or which direction she was even facing.

Another hit to the back, and Sadie swore violently, fear rushing through her. She yanked the wheel, and her truck swerved to the side of the road, bouncing over packed snow.

Her stomach dropped. This was going to be bad, she realized. The truck was hurtling toward a steep drop-off. Sadie tried to turn, to steer the truck into the snow so that she could, at least, put a stop to this out of control nightmare.

But it didn't work; the snow was loosely packed, and the truck simply forged through, now gaining more speed. She was racing downhill, a passenger in her truck as it lurched and skidded.

She was desperately braking, now, praying her truck wouldn't slide any further. Praying it would stop. But it didn't, and now the cab was looming in her mirror again.

The cab hit her again, surging forward and smashing into the back of Sadie's truck.

And this time, it tipped her over the edge, literally.

Sadie felt a stomach-lurching moment where her truck lifted off the road. She was airborne for long, terrifying seconds as she plummeted downwards.

And then, she was in freefall, plunging down a sharp drop she hadn't even known about, invisible in the white-out.

Her truck bounced, rolled, and bounced again, the vehicle she was trapped inside now a dangerous projectile.

Sadie was knocked forward, her seatbelt cutting into her as her truck flipped onto its side.

She tried to clutch the steering wheel, tried to grab a hold of something that would break her fall and kill the momentum but she was rammed forward by another shockwave. The air bags burst in her face.

She hit the slope at the bottom of the ravine with a jarring impact, feeling the back of her truck crunch and crumple. She rolled again, and then finally slammed to a motionless stop.

Collapsing back against her seat, Sadie was aware of a ringing in her ears. She was shaking, her heart racing. She could hear her breath, harsh in the sudden silence, as she got her bearings and tried to work out where this new disaster had landed her.

Her truck was wedged at an angle, hood-up in the snow. She could see the faint shape of a tree to her right. She automatically reached for the door, but realized that if she opened it, she'd fall out into the snow.

Cursing, she fumbled with the seatbelt, trying to loosen it because it might have saved her during the fall, but now it was trapping her. She felt a sense of desperation that she'd lost this fight, that she would take hours to get back to the road, and that by then, Joanie and her prisoner would be long gone.

Frantically, she yanked at the belt, and finally managed to tug it loose.

And then, from above, Sadie heard a noise that she couldn't place at first.

It was a scraping, rumbling noise that brought to mind the sliding rocks of an avalanche. What was it, she wondered, as a chunk of snow fell onto the roof of her truck, and she heard a scream of metal from above.

And then, with a gasp, she realized.

Joanie hadn't avoided the drop. She hadn't kept control of her cab in the icy conditions. The slippery slope that had claimed Sadie had claimed her, too.

Now, the cab was plunging down the snowy slope, and she realized that, channeled by the narrowness of this crevasse, it must be on a direct collision course with Sadie's car.

She heard metal shriek again. She could see the dark shape of the cab through her cracked windshield, looming above her head, falling rapidly.

If she didn't get out of the car, and out of the way, she was going to be crushed when the heavy cab plowed down the slope.

She had only a moment to save her own life.

CHAPTER TWENTY SIX

With a gasp, Sadie reached for the door. She wrenched it open and tumbled out, rolling into the snow. She tried to get to her feet, but slipped and fell, skidding down the icy slope.

She flinched as, from above, she heard a rending crash, the horrible sound of metal ripping into metal. The cab was plummeting down the snowy crevasse, jolting and twisting as it fell, and although it looked to be on a collision course for her truck, it could also ricochet and end up colliding with her.

The next moments were all about survival, nothing more.

She scrambled out of the way, seeing a narrow nook in the rock, wedging herself into it in the hope that the overhang would protect her as the cab smashed down.

As the cab bounced down the slope, Sadie felt a rush of air as it flew toward her. The cab was coming closer, sliding down the slope, she could actually see its undercarriage, now dented and crumpled, but still rolling inexorably in her direction.

She closed her eyes, gasping, arms over her head, willing herself to be protected by the overhang. She felt a whooshing noise as something heavy whipped past her.

And then, there was a screeching grind as metal scraped against metal. The sound of twisting, an unnatural tearing and crunching sound as metal folded and crumpled.

She heard the crash, felt it rumble through the ground, and then silence fell. She opened her eyes.

The cab had landed on her truck, its chassis wedged against her back bumper, denting it severely and wedging her truck deep into the snow-covered fissure.

The cab's engine was still racing, hissing, and steaming in the snow.

What about the occupants?

Sadie waited, crouched in the snow.

When she was sure the cab was stable, and wasn't going to tip and crush her, she edged out of her hiding place.

With her gun drawn, she clambered out of the rocky nook and crept closer, wondering if there was any way that Joanie and her hostage could have survived this fall.

She caught her breath, seeing movement from inside the cab. And then, the door flew open.

Hissing in a breath, Sadie steadied her gun, but then hesitated.

Joanie was in the doorway, with the hostage trapped in her grasp. She had her arm wedged tightly around the terrified woman's neck, and she had a short, sharp utility knife pressed to her throat.

The hostage looked unharmed, Sadie saw, but terrified. Joanie herself had a graze on her cheek, and her hair had worked loose from what Sadie guessed was its trademark braid. Now, it wisped around her face, tangled and wild, and Sadie could clearly see the madness in her eyes.

The hostage, a plump, blue-eyed woman who looked in her mid-twenties, was clearly terrified. Frozen in her captor's grasp, she stared at Sadie in silent appeal, her breathing hoarse from under the tight, merciless grip.

She was about ten yards away from Joanie, Sadie calculated. It was too far to risk taking a shot. Their heads were too close, and Joanie's body was fully shielded by her hostage.

Every moment, every movement, every decision that Sadie now made would count. And the wrong decision could cost the hostage's life.

Joanie was breathing hard, staring at Sadie with narrowed eyes. And just as Sadie was wondering what the best way of solving this impasse would be, to her shock, Joanie spoke.

Her voice was harsh and husky, the way that she remembered her sounding yesterday.

"Well, that was clever of you. Now look what you've done. You got us both off the road there. Why didn't you just let me be?"

She spoke surprisingly casually. Her voice didn't sound at all like the voice of a woman who'd just been on a careening hell ride down a ravine. It sounded impossibly calm, and as she listened to her, Sadie realized that she was staring into the narrowed blue eyes of a true psychopath, someone whose emotions didn't function in the normal spectrum at all. No wonder she'd been able to do what she did so calmly.

What Sadie didn't know was how to respond to her. Calculated and calm as she was, she had no doubt that she was biding her time before flaring into a killing rage. Which she would probably do once Sadie had provided her with a trigger.

No triggers, then, Sadie thought.

Keeping an eye on Joanie's knife, she said, "You need to let this woman go. She's done nothing. There's no need for her to be caught up in this."

"Oh, yes, there is. I took her for a reason." Joanie's smile flashed, cold and mirthless. "You know what the reason is if you're here, I guess, cop woman. Finally got it right this time? You weren't so clever yesterday, were you?"

Keep her talking, that was the only thing she could do, Sadie decided. There was no other way of buying time. She had her gun and although she couldn't use it now, she might be able to if Joanie gave her a gap. Time might work on her side here. Joanie might shift, allowing her a clear shot.

Joanie's arms might get tired of pinning the hostage in place, although she could see the wiry power in her grasp.

Or the cold might get to both of them, Sadie realized with a shiver. And down in this ravine, although they were sheltered from the blasting wind, the temperature was still way below freezing.

"No, I wasn't so clever yesterday. You were definitely smarter than me." She saw the flash of triumph in Joanie's eyes at this praise. Sadie recalled that many psychopaths had egos, and Joanie was definitely in their numbers.

"But why are you doing this? What is making you do it?" Sadie then asked, doing her best to keep a conversational tone and to keep the stress and tension out of her voice, because she had a sense they might trigger her adversary.

"The weak must die, and only the strong survive," Joanie said with an evil grin. "That's my job. My calling. It's what my mother always taught me, and she taught me the hard way, with no pity. No mercy. She died a couple of months ago, and it took me a while to get my head around it." Joanie briefly shook her head, as if banishing bad memories.

Sadie was now sure that Joanie herself had suffered abuse at her mother's hands, and that this was partially responsible for her becoming the monster she was. Undoubtedly her mother's death had provided the trigger for Joanie to begin killing. She must see herself as continuing her mother's work, Sadie realized.

"So now, I am doing the same. I am making sure that the weak women get annihilated," Joanie further explained.

"Do you really hate women that much?" Sadie asked quietly.

"Yes. I hate them." Joanie sneered, then added, her voice full of disgust, "They're nothing but whores and gold diggers. I hate them, but the weak are the worst. They deserve to die, and then to be dumped somewhere, like trash."

Sadie realized that in this make or break scenario, she was running out of time. And it wasn't because of Joanie. It was because of the hostage. Sadie could see her face. She could see that her eyes were starting to flicker, and to roll up in her head. Although she was managing to stay on her feet by an effort of will, she was very close to blacking out.

Joanie couldn't see Louise's face. Sadie could.

This would give her an opportunity. When the hostage collapsed, she would have a chance.

She could rush the other woman as she struggled with the sudden dead weight in her arms.

Keep her talking in the meantime, Sadie resolved.

"You seem to be doing that just fine," Sadie said carefully. "Why did you make the call to the hotline, though?"

That had been what clued her to Joanie's identity.

"I wanted to frame that driver. That piece of trash. I knew he'd take the fall for it while I escaped. Because I will escape," she threatened. "I'll get across the border and disappear forever. You won't stop me. I'll kill you. And you're dead meat, sweetheart," she hissed into the hostage's ear.

At that moment, Sadie saw the light leave the hostage's eyes and she knew that Louise was going to black out.

This was her moment.

It might be the only break that she could use. She had to make the most of it. And then, Louise collapsed, causing Joanie to stagger.

Immediately, praying this would work, Sadie rushed forward.

CHAPTER TWENTY SEVEN

As she lunged toward Joanie, Sadie saw immediately that her plan was not going to work. Because Joanie was too quick. Frighteningly fast. As soon as she felt the other woman's dead weight in her hands and saw Sadie lunge toward her, Joanie reacted faster than Sadie had believed possible.

She dropped Louise, who sprawled on the snow, and then she jumped forward, ducking under Sadie's outstretched arm even as she aimed her gun. In a flash, with a strength that Sadie hadn't believed possible, Joanie's left hand grabbed Sadie's right and she twisted her wrist, digging her fingers in, fighting to get control of that gun. At the same time, Sadie had to duck away from a savage thrusts of the knife in Joanie's right hand.

The grip of her fingers was too sudden, too intense, and Sadie knew there was only one way to try and fight this battle. Her wrist was being cruelly twisted and there was no way of dislodging the other woman's grip.

So instead, regretting her action, knowing she was all out of other choices, she dropped her own gun and kicked it away, hearing Joanie snarl in rage. But at least her grip loosened and Sadie was able to wrench her arm away, her wrist throbbing.

Then Sadie desperately tried to defend herself against that flashing blade.

Joanie was on the attack, moving with the swiftness of a striking snake. Sadie managed to jump back, leaping away, avoiding a slashing attack by Joanie's blade and then ducking down to avoid a second one.

The two women grappled, and Sadie struggled to escape the deadly blade. She was worried she wouldn't be able to avoid it for long, because Joanie wasn't going to give her the chance. She was tall, and probably forty pounds heavier than Sadie. Her strength was overpowering, and she was fast with it, too.

She was giving Sadie no room or time to dodge the knife. It flashed again and again, and Sadie felt a tearing rip as it caught the sleeve of her jacket. It ripped through the cloth and she felt a light sting where the sharp blade had gashed her skin.

Joanie was already lunging at her again, and even as Sadie threw herself back, her foot slipped, and she went down on her knees. But she was still able to twist away from that knife, and to swing her arm up at Joanie's legs.

Joanie was again too quick for her. She jumped away, and in that split second Sadie saw that a full-blown rage was now burning in her eyes. Her emotions were out of control.

In an instant, Joanie leapt at her again, her face contorted with fury, her arm raised with the knife.

Sadie lunged, desperately trying to get a hold of the other woman's swinging arm, but it was impossible. She ducked out of the way, sprawling back as the knife flashed down and Joanie gave a gasping laugh before moving in for a fresh attack.

Surely this woman was not a machine, surely there must be some weakness, some vulnerability that she could use to give herself a fighting chance?

As Sadie braced herself, moving swiftly back as she tried to balance in the slippery, snowy terrain, she realized what her only hope was. She could see that Joanie's shoulders were heaving. Although she was strong and fast, she was not fit. She was, after all, a trucker who spent long hours behind the wheel. She was going to tire quicker than Sadie, and if Sadie could avoid the knife for long enough, then she might get the chance she needed.

She needed something more, though, a weapon. Her gun was gone, it had tumbled into the snow. But if she could work her way around to the truck's cab, she might find something in there.

She was also being worn down by this fight. As she scrambled back, writhing out of reach, she knew that this combat, in the icy cold, was also taking its toll on her.

"Come to me, bitch!" Joanie yelled. "Come to me and I'll cut you down to size."

Snow whirled down, pouring into the ravine. From above, she could hear the howl of the incessant wind.

Sadie ducked under the woman's slashing arm, then rolled back. She was close to the cab now, close to that open door. But as she reached it, Joanie stabbed again, and this time, the blade thrust into Sadie's left arm and she gasped as pain lanced through her. Almost immediately, she felt her sleeve, wet and warm with blood.

Joanie's triumphant cry proved to Sadie that she'd seen blood, and that this show of weakness was now triggering her to kill.

The desperation of her situation spurred her on. With a last burst of speed, Sadie lunged to the right, and grabbed the doorframe even as her feet skidded in the snow. Her left hand could barely hold on. Her arm was stinging with pain, and the gash was bleeding freely.

Yelling, Sadie kicked out as Joanie used the moment to attack again. Her foot caught the woman a glancing blow, squarely on the kneecap, enough to send her sprawling down with an angry cry.

And then, Sadie was scrabbling in the truck cab, looking for a weapon to use, anything that could help. There was a cellphone there, but the screen was smashed to smithereens. Cash strewn below the passenger seat. A couple of burger wrappers. Maps and notebooks from the man Joanie had stolen it from, whose life was inside here.

And a weapon, one she could use. There it was. The tire iron. Grisly, heavy, its tip still stained darkly with blood.

She grasped it in her right hand, twisting around, knowing that she had one chance, and only one, to launch this counter attack.

She saw Joanie bucking to her feet, a hand clutching her knee and her eyes burning with fury. In her hand, Sadie saw the knife flash, and she knew that this was it.

She had to go for it.

Lashing out with her leg, she kicked the knife aside, thrusting out with the sole of her boot with all her remaining strength to deflect the blade. And finally, her tiring adversary showed signs of weakness, stumbling back her arms flailing as she lost her balance in the snow.

Sadie raised the tire iron, and a cry of effort burst from her lips as she brought it down onto Joanie's head.

With a sickening, hollow crack, the tire iron smashed into her head.

Joanie fell to her knees. Her eyes rolled back in her head. She dropped her knife. She swayed. And then she fell, sprawling down into the snow.

Her chest was still heaving. She was knocked out, but she wasn't dead. Working as fast as she could, Sadie dragged her into the truck's sleeper cab. It took all her strength to manhandle this woman's dead weight into the cab, especially with an incapacitated left hand. But she had to. Leaving her outside in this cold meant leaving her to certain death. She deserved to face her crimes and to receive the cold justice of the law, and a life in prison.

Finally, Sadie got her inside and firmly handcuffed with her hands behind her and her legs tied.

Then, she rushed back, gasping for breath, to get Louise, who was in tears, but conscious again. She helped Louise to the truck and got her into the passenger seat.

Then, with her strength now entirely sapped, Sadie scrambled into the driver's seat on legs that felt boneless. She was utterly spent, and her arm was in agony.

She slammed the door and cranked the heater up as high as it would go. She didn't know how long the fuel would last, or if the storm and the cold would kill them. She didn't know if the combined weight of the vehicles would slide deeper into the ravine, making it impossible for them to open the doors again at all.

But those factors were beyond her control now, and she had no more strength left. She'd done what she could, and now their survival was out of her hands.

She thought of Cooper again, mouthing his name silently. Then, collapsing over the steering wheel, darkness enfolded her.

CHAPTER TWENTY EIGHT

State Trooper Cowell felt sick with anxiety. This was the most stressful outcome to a case he'd ever known. Not that there was an actual outcome, because nobody had been found.

Was Agent Sadie Price still alive?

Or had the scenario happened that he feared the most, and had the woman he respected lost her life in the storm?

Now, standing at the door to the Tok police department where he'd spent an uncomfortable night on the floor in a spare sleeping bag, feeling fraught with worry, he waited for the dispatch unit to be ready to go out.

It was eight am, the storm had finally blown over, and Cowell acknowledged what terrible timing it had been. The white-out had shut down the area, bringing all operations to a grinding halt, making cellphone communication impossible. Now, signal was up again at last.

They were sending a convoy of cars out on the Taylor Highway to search for her. A search and rescue operation. Cowell had also requested a helicopter, but in the mayhem following the storm, he'd been told that helicopter services were not available. There were only a few choppers in the area and they were all already booked up for the day in various search and rescue efforts.

Cowell tried yet again to call Sadie, grimacing as the call went to voicemail. The fact there was still no connection to her phone was a huge worry. Would they be able to find her if her phone had been destroyed, if the battery had died, if she'd run off the road and crashed. Being stuck in the cold for so long would have been lethal, he had no doubt.

Or worse still, had the killer found her? That was another serious possibility. Especially since the hostage, Louise, was also out of contact.

Worst case scenarios flooded his mind.

Swallowing down his worry, Cowell realized that the convoy was ready to head out at last.

"Let's get going," the lead trooper said, a tall, blonde man called Officer Steiner, who'd arrived to take charge. At least they had some manpower and cars - four cars in total, that would be able to search the highway now that the storm had abated.

Plows had been clearing the highway, but the snowplow drivers had reported no sign of her.

It was still bitterly cold, but the sky was a freezing blue after the clouds had passed over.

Cowell climbed in his car, listening to the crackle of the radio as the team communicated their strategy.

It was a good plan. They would start at the entrance to the highway, the one that led onto the Taylor Highway. Then, they'd head north, and stop every mile or so to check the road and the snow banks.

Cowell felt a knot in his stomach. The signs weren't good. With the amount of snow that had fallen, would an accident even be noticed?

He knew the chances of them still being alive were dwindling with every second that passed. And from the team's grim faces, he knew the others knew it too.

The convoy pulled off. Cowell was riding second in line, behind Steiner.

They moved out slowly, and Cowell knew that this search was going to take them a while. In the back of his mind, he worried that they would miss her entirely.

Was she already dead? He didn't want to think about that. In the short time he'd known Sadie Price, she'd impressed him in so many ways. With her forthright attitude, her courage, her capability, her integrity, and her smarts, she had made him want to be a better cop himself. She was so strong, so full of life energy. It seemed impossibly cruel that the deadly combination of a storm and a killer could have put out her spark.

Cowell drove, following Steiner, his mind whirling with the possible scenarios.

They headed out onto the highway, tires skimming across the clear blacktop, aware that the piles of snow on either side represented formidable barriers. This was going to take some scrambling and climbing.

Ahead, he saw a vehicle approaching. Was it a snowplow?

No. Squinting into the low morning sun, he saw it was not a snowplow but in fact, a yellow backhoe.

A yellow backhoe was puttering along the highway in their direction. And then, Cowell's pulse accelerated as the convoy neared the vehicle. Disbelief and joy warred inside him as he took in the impossible, yet amazing sight.

Sadie Price was at the controls, her face pale and grim, but intent, her clothes bloodstained. She looked as if she was at the end of her strength, running on empty, her face bloodied and grim, but she was alive, at least. He guessed something must have happened to her truck. She must have gotten that backhoe off of the trailer that the killer stole, he realized, and used it as a viable form of transport. That meant she must have caught up with the killer!

And then he saw that sitting beside her, looking shell shocked but unharmed, was Louise, the cashier from the Tok truck stop.

"They've done it!" His cry of triumph resounded around the car. "They've done it! Call off the search. We need to get them to the hospital, urgently."

CHAPTER TWENTY NINE

Sadie couldn't believe that she'd made it. The hospital room seemed like the warmest, most luxurious hotel she'd ever been in. Every time she closed her eyes, visions of the ordeal loomed. The fight she'd been through. The blowing snow. The stomach-churning freefall when her car had been pushed off the road.

And the fight to the death with the killer. She shivered all over again. Even though Joanie was now firmly locked in a prison cell, with no chance of ever seeing the light of day as a free woman again, Sadie knew that the memories of that terrifying fight would take a while to subside.

But at least she'd done it. Joanie would never kill again. The final hostage had been saved. And the case had been closed.

In a way she couldn't believe it, and perhaps what convinced her the most that this really was over, were the waves of emotion that now kept swirling around her as she allowed herself, finally, to process the tragedy of what had happened to her mother - and most probably, Jessica, too.

For about the tenth time that day, Sadie closed her eyes, seeking refuge in the darkness as tears flowed, tears that felt as if they had been held inside her for years. Decades, even. The process of allowing herself to grieve was painful, but it was also cathartic.

"Agent Price."

The voice jolted her out of her musings and Sadie quickly snapped her eyes open.

It was the ward doctor speaking. The slim man, about thirty years old, had treated her wounds expertly yesterday, but had refused to discharge her, saying she needed to rest up, that she was suffering from exhaustion and exposure and that hospital was the best place for her.

Now, she looked at him warily. Was he going to make her spend more time here? She was feeling well now. Her energy had returned.

And clearly, the doc felt the same, nodding approvingly as he read her charts.

"You're cleared to go. You are fully stabilized, and you've made an excellent recovery overnight. You'll just need to get those stitches in your arm removed in a week or so. And there are some colleagues waiting for you at the entrance to the ward."

"Thanks, doc," she said, feeling pleased. She hoped that State Trooper Cowell would be waiting. She wanted to say a proper goodbye to him before heading home, and thank him for everything he'd done. He'd been a great partner, brave and positive. She couldn't have asked for a better companion in the hunt for a lethal killer.

Carefully, she got out of bed, wincing as her now-stiff muscles swung into action. Grabbing her things, moving with caution thanks to her bandaged left arm, she headed for the bathroom to get changed.

As she walked out of the bathroom, her phone rang. It was Golightly calling. Quickly, Sadie picked it up.

"Sadie? I hope you're recovered from yesterday," Golightly said, and she could hear the anxiety in his voice.

"The doc's just given me the all-clear," she told him, feeling relieved all over again that she'd made it.

"I'm glad to hear that. You're booked off for the next two weeks. Take a vacation. You deserve it, and you need the time for your arm to heal. I don't want you back on duty until it's better, and you're fully healed up."

"Thank you," Sadie said gratefully.

"When you get back, we need to have a talk," he said, his voice loaded with meaning, and Sadie nodded to herself. They did need to talk. About her future, and the offer he'd made her to take up the post of Senior Agent.

"I'll look forward to that," she said, smiling. She felt surer now about what her answer would be.

After cutting the call, she walked out of the ward and headed for the reception area.

There, she stopped, feeling shocked and delighted as Sheriff Cooper, sitting next to Cowell, got up from the plastic seat and walked over, his strong face alight, his eyes shining with warmth.

"Cooper!" she said.

She didn't have time for more as his arms enfolded her, wrapping her in a gentle but strong embrace. She felt a rush of pure happiness to be loved, that there was someone who had cared enough about her to have done this, to have driven here. For her.

And she would have done the same for him, she realized now.

"I can't believe you came all the way out here," she said.

"Well, I had to," he replied gruffly, with a note of humor to his voice. "I got a message that you'd driven your car off the road and smashed it up some. Figured you'd need wheels to get back home."

Sadie snorted, feeling tears threaten again, but this time, for sure, they were tears of happiness.

"It's good to see you," she whispered.

"And you. Well done. This case was a shocker. I'm sure you've been through hell. I'm just glad you made it out the other side, and got the killer along the way." She could hear the worry resonating in his tone.

"I've got some vacation due. I've been booked off work for two weeks," she told him.

"Good. You need to recover, and perhaps to spend time shopping for a new vehicle," he said wryly.

Finally ending the hug, Sadie turned to Cowell.

"Thank you for everything," she said. "You've been great. I hope I can work with you again sometime."

"Me, too," the young trooper said, looking proud. "I've learned so much in the past few days. I - er - well, it's been an honor," he stammered out, blushing.

Feeling a rush of friendship for this likable and passionate young man, Sadie hugged him, too.

"Keep in touch," she warned him.

"I will. And you too, please," he replied.

And then, she walked downstairs with Cooper, heading for his sheriff's truck which was parked outside the hospital entrance.

"I can't believe this is over," Sadie said, feeling exhausted, relieved, and satisfied.

"You did a good job, Sadie. I'm happy to have you back in one piece."

Sadie gave a weary smile, feeling so grateful for the warmth and support that Cooper was showing her.

"Vacation means just that, vacation," Cooper warned. Perhaps he'd seen the look in Sadie's eyes as those memories surged yet again. "You need to spend some downtime, to process everything that's happened."

She knew he'd seen her face and had accurately guessed the direction in which her thoughts had veered. Continuing, Cooper said, "Caz said Jenny's on vacation from school now, and she needs someone to do activities with her."

Sadie's mind veered away from the sensitive topic of her mother, back to the far happier thoughts of how good it would be to see Caz again, and what she and Jenny could get up to.

"And I'm going to request the pleasure of your company for dinner tonight," Cooper warned. "And tomorrow night."

"And the night after that?" Sadie joked. "Would you consider a dinner date with me?"

"I might just have a gap in my schedule," Cooper assured her, his face deadpan.

They climbed into the car and he started it up, setting off along the cleared roads, with the sun blazing down, almost blinding against the icy, white, newly fallen snow.

As Cooper headed away from the hospital, Sadie turned and glanced back at it. She had been so lucky to survive. And now, she was free to travel home with the Sheriff and spend some quality time with Caz.

She felt a warm glow inside her, and the last of the emotional tears that had been threatening the past few days and hours, finally began to flow.

She turned her face to the window, looking out, not wanting Cooper to see her crying, and feeling glad of the sunglasses that hid what she was feeling inside.

Sadie wept for her mother, and for her sister.

And as she wept, she knew that, although it was necessary to recuperate and she would respect Cooper's pleas that she must take downtime to mentally and physically heal herself, Sadie promised that it would not be for too long.

As soon as she was feeling stronger again, when her arm had healed and she was rested, she was going to continue her research.

She was going to find out exactly where Burt McAfee lived. Someone in town would know, or some old record would point the way to his location, once she had time to search. And she was going to drive out there, into the icy hinterland, and confront him. He'd taken a life for a life, he'd murdered her mother and her sister, but he could not hide away from justice, or from her, any longer.

McAfee's day of reckoning would come. And Sadie promised herself that it was not far away.

CHAPTER THIRTY

The road that Sadie and Cooper were driving along was narrow and rough, nothing more than a fire road, almost impassable in places. The truck jolted and bounced as Cooper eased it over the worst of the ruts, avoiding the packed snow and the hidden rocks. Around them, the landscape was desolate and bleak.

Sadie felt cold inside with anticipation.

If their reckoning was right, and the research she and Cooper had done over the past week was correct, then this was the road that led to Burt McAfee's cabin. An old delivery note from the local hardware store had eventually confirmed the location. It seemed he'd renovated the cabin about ten years ago and had gotten a few materials sent out there.

"Are you ready?" Cooper asked her.

She looked at him. He was driving with calm concentration, his hands gripping the steering wheel as he navigated the harsh terrain. He was focused on his own job, on finding Burt McAfee, confronting him and bringing him down.

"I'm ready," she said.

And she was.

She'd waited a week before driving out here, using the time to heal. But now, she could wait no longer. She was going to demand answers from him - answers about her mother, and also answers about Jessica. Where had she disappeared to? Had McAfee murdered her too? Sadie was sure the answer was yes. She was sure that this brutal man had claimed two lives in his quest for justice as he perceived it.

A life for a life. Two lives for two.

The knowledge ate away at Sadie, filling her with a deep regret that she had not been able to stop this catastrophe from playing out. Years later, too little, too late, all she could do was follow the trail and try to make sure that McAfee paid for what he'd done.

In a hard society, she had learned that he had been one of the most brutal men, with a reputation that preceded him.

He was responsible for her mother's death. Without a doubt, she knew this. But what about her sister?

She dreaded the answer, but knew it was time to learn it.

"There it is." Cooper slowed the truck. He pointed to a cabin, over a ridge ahead, almost hidden by the trees. "It's the only building out here. It must be his," he said.

"It must be," Sadie agreed.

Now that she was here, and actually ready to confront this man, her mouth felt dry and her stomach was churning. She didn't know how this scene would play out. But she felt, with a sense of doom, that there could surely be no good conclusion.

She felt grateful beyond words for Cooper's strong, supportive presence beside her.

Then Cooper braked sharply, tires skidding as he wrenched the wheel. Sadie stared at the trench in the road that he'd narrowly avoided getting stuck in. Floodwater had eroded it into a steep fissure. There was no way that a car could get over this.

"I guess we go on foot from here," she said.

They climbed out. The air felt cold and still. The stitches in her arm had been removed yesterday, but it was still tender and weaker than it should be. But for now, she was able to clamber down the ditch, holding it carefully, and scramble up the other side, grabbing Cooper's hand to help her up the steep section.

And then they continued on foot, their steps crunching over the loose rocks and drifting snow.

Approaching McAfee's home, Sadie saw the cabin was small, compact, and very solid looking, though deeply weathered. There were two windows, one on each side, and a small, narrow door in the middle.

Breathing deeply, Sadie tried to control her emotions. She felt afraid of what she would find. And yet, she needed to find out the truth.

"I guess we'd better do this," she said.

"Right," Cooper said.

Sadie strode up to the front door, pretending a confidence she didn't feel inside, and hammered on it.

She waited. And a few moments later, it opened. Her heart sped up as the hinges squealed and the door juddered wide, as if the old wood was protesting.

There was McAfee, staring at her.

Sadie had expected to feel a wave of hatred, of loathing for him. But instead, she felt surprise. He looked so much older, so much frailer than she'd expected. He was a wizened, gray-haired husk of a man and she wondered immediately if he was healthy, or if there was something, some illness or disease, eating away at him. He was wrapped in a weathered parka, but under it, she could see his body was frail, all sharp angles.

Only his eyes were bright and alert as he stared at them coldly.

Burt McAfee. The man who had hunted her down and murdered her mother. The man she was sure had killed her sister, too.

"Good morning," he said. His voice was dry and breathy. "What are you doing here?"

There was no time for social niceties. Sadie got straight to the point, a flame of resolve driving her forward.

"Mr. McAfee. I'm FBI Agent Sadie Price. With me is Sheriff Cooper. We're here to get answers. There's strong evidence that you killed my mother. Her remains have been found. It's been confirmed as murder. So it's an open case, and you're a suspect."

He pinched his wizened lips together, staring from one of them to the other.

"All right," he said. "You're here. Now what?"

"I want the truth."

He uttered a dry laugh. "You police are all the same. You say you want the truth. But that's never all you want. There are always strings attached. You'll take a man's life, you'll take his soul."

"Did you take a life?" Sadie demanded, even though this conversation was strangely chilling. "My mother's?"

He stared at her with a calculating gaze, as if wondering what to say. And then he nodded.

"I did. I killed her."

"Why?" The word burst out of Sadie's mouth, her tone anguished.

"You know why," McAfee replied calmly. "You know why or you wouldn't be here now. It was because she killed my wife and my daughter. She was responsible for the death of my family, in childbirth. You have no idea of the pain I felt."

"If you felt such pain, why did you want to cause it to an innocent family?" Sadie agonized to him. "My mother tried her hardest to save your wife. Circumstances wouldn't allow it. She couldn't access the medical help she needed."

Sadie took a deep breath. Blame, now, was futile, and she had the sense this man was impervious to guilt. Now, she needed to get more answers. The ones she'd come here for.

"So you took her life," she added. "Because of the death of your wife. But what about my sister? What did you do to her? Did you kill Jessica too?"

"You have no sister. That I know."

"You're lying," Cooper interrupted.

McAfee shrugged. His gaze slid away.

"I don't know what you're talking about," he said.

Cooper moved forward. Sadie could tell he was angry and impatient, but he kept his voice under control.

"You know who we mean. We didn't come here for you to play games. If you didn't kill her sister, then what happened to her?"

McAfee sighed.

"You really want to know? It might not be the answer you want. It might not be the answer you like. If I was you, I'd leave it be. I'd get the hell out of here and be satisfied with what you have already."

Sadie hissed in a breath.

"I want the answer. I don't care what it is. Now tell me, McAfee. What happened to her? Because I know you played a part in this. You can't deny it!"

"Alright." He nodded, capitulating at last, as if her own resolve had stormed through his resistance. "You're not going to like the answer. But I'll tell you."

CHAPTER THIRTY ONE

"Your father gave her to me," McAfee hissed to Sadie, his eyes gleaming, the words erupting from his mouth, harsh and shocking. "He gave her to me, to raise as my own for three years. We all knew it was an unbreakable deal."

She gasped. Beside her, she felt Cooper tense, drawing in a shocked breath.

"What? That's impossible!"

McAfee shook his head. "It's what happened. You see, I gave your dad a choice. After I'd killed your mother, I thought it would be enough. That I'd had my payback. But it wasn't enough, and I got angrier and angrier about it, over the years, seeing that your family was still whole and mine was broken, with nothing left for me, ever. Eventually, I told him that I wanted justice. No, in fact, that I demanded justice."

"In what way?" Sadie asked, her mouth dry.

"I wanted him to lose a child, too, so I told him to hand one of his daughters over to me. And I told him it had to be her. I knew she was his favorite. That losing her would hurt him more."

McAfee's chin jutted stubbornly.

Sadie felt shock ricochet through her - most of all, because she didn't doubt the truth of the words. They were spoken from the heart, she sensed. This bitter, murderous old man was all done with lies.

"And my dad agreed to this?" she said incredulously.

Her own father had given her sister over to this violent man, this killer? Had sacrificed her? She simply could not believe the extent of this betrayal. And how could he have done such a thing when Jessica had been his favorite?

McAfee shrugged. "He didn't want to. Nor did she. But he had no choice. Neither of them did."

"Why's that?" Sadie shivered. This was a full confession. They had McAfee. Late in time as it was, this was the end of his life as a free man. He was going to go down for murder. But before that, she wanted all the answers, all the reasons, while standing here, breathing in the cold air outside this battered cabin that had been home to a murderer for decades.

"Because I told him that if he didn't agree, he was going to lose both his children. And he knew that I'd do it." Now there was a threatening tone to his words. "He knew my family, he knew the power we held. He had no doubt about that. None at all."

Sadie felt at a loss for words.

Her sister, Jessica, had agreed to this in order to save Sadie from this monster. To keep Sadie alive, she'd gone willingly to this cabin, to live here in the remote wilderness, with this angry, abusive man?

She'd done it for Sadie.

If this was true, how was she going to live with the guilt that her sister had lived through hell? And where was Jessica now? Had he ended up killing her?

She drew in a breath to ask, but he raised a gnarled hand, his finger in the air. "I made your father promise not to tell. I said if he told, if this had consequences for me, there'd be consequences for him, too. There was some other woman who drowned in the lake. He pretended those remains must be Jessica's. But she was here, with me. For four years, she was my daughter."

"And then? Did you kill her?" Sadie spat.

"Why would I do that?" McAfee replied calmly. "I treated her well. I cared for her as if she was my own. We had four happy years. As happy as they could be, under the circumstances," he remembered. "When she was twenty-one, she left, for San Francisco, I think. I don't think she contacted anyone from town. That was part of the deal. You'd gone by then, anyway. She knew you'd be able to escape your father, and she never wanted to speak to him again. So she kept her side of the bargain. For you."

"The bargain?" Sadie said in shock. She still had no idea if she believed him. Was this all a lie? This was the most terrible trade-off she'd ever heard of. To protect her, her sister had disappeared, spending four precious years of her life in this monster's clutches?

"She changed her name. I called her Belinda."

"Belinda?"

"Jessica Price was thought to be dead. Perhaps your father even certified her dead? So yes, she had to have a new name. A new start. That was the name my wife and I had chosen for my daughter. Your father even signed a document agreeing to it. I'll show you."

"You signed a contract?" Sadie said in disbelief. "Why would my father do that?"

"Oh, he also wanted to make sure nobody would find out what he'd done. Don't think he didn't feel guilty about wrongly identifying a body, and trading one daughter to ensure the life of both. He knew how that would look."

"You'd better get it quick," Sadie threatened. "Because we're bringing you in, regardless."

He turned and limped into the cabin. Sadie waited. Her heart was pounding so loud she could hear it in her own ears. She glanced at Cooper, seeing that he looked as appalled as she felt.

But then, they both jumped, as from inside the cabin, a shot rang out.

"No!" Sadie yelled. She burst through the doorway and into the gloomy interior. "No, no!"

But it was too late. McAfee lay dead on the floorboards, blood oozing from the wound in his temple, the gun by his side.

Crouching to the floor, Sadie checked his pulse, her own heart hammering, but it was too late. He was gone.

Tears flooded her eyes.

"I don't believe this!"

Sadie felt her breath coming in gasps. He'd outwitted them, escaped them, just as they were about to bring him to justice.

And was the contract real, or just an excuse to leave them waiting while he went back inside to get his gun?

Her father would never have signed such a thing. Or would he? After all, Sadie had thought he'd never have given one of his own children away, and look what had happened.

The thought crossed her mind that perhaps her father hadn't had a choice. He'd sacrificed one child to save the other from a man who was outspokenly murderous and had already killed, in a remote and lawless society. Nobody messed with the McAfees. Nobody. She knew that, and without a doubt, her father and Jessica had known that too.

Whatever the terms were, they could have been forced to agree, knowing that any other decision would have meant both Jessica and Sadie died. And that must have been why Jessica never tried to contact her again, knowing it was the only way, for both of them.

"We can search the place," Cooper said, his calm voice grounding her again. "Perhaps there's some evidence. Something that can give us a lead as to the truth of all of this."

Clambering to her feet, dizzy with shock, Sadie nodded. This was their only answer now. The evidence that McAfee had left behind - if any - was now their only recourse in learning the full truth.

Stepping carefully away from the body, frail and small in death, Sadie moved to the back of the cabin. There were two bedrooms, one empty, with only a narrow single bed, and the other clearly where McAfee had lived. It was musty smelling, but neat and clean. There were folders, old letters, boxes of documents and trinkets. Old boxes of ammunition.

An agreement? Would such a thing be found here, Sadie wondered.

"Do you think he was telling the truth?" Sadie asked, hearing the incredulity in her own voice.

Because, if he was, then he'd given her a surge of unwanted hope. That Jessica, under her new name, was still alive.

"Let's look," Cooper said.

They pulled out the files, placed them on the bed.

Sadie opened them, paging through, but they seemed to be random collections of documents, old notes, faded items that looked years old. And an envelope that had something in.

Photographs, Sadie saw, shaking them out. Not a contract.

She took a closer look, her eyes narrowing.

"Cooper!" she said. "Look! Look here!"

The photos were of Jessica, undoubtedly. Standing outside this cabin, framed by this view.

They were old and blurred, taken by a cheap camera, but as she stared at them anxiously, Sadie didn't think that her sister looked unhappy.

"It's her!" Sadie felt sobs erupting again.

Her mind went back to the way that McAfee's criminal activities, his violent tendencies, had seemed to curb themselves and disappear off the radar in later years. There had been no more convictions – not from Burt, at any rate.

Was it possible that, with the care of her sister, he'd forced himself away from his path in life and become a better person? Was it possible that her sister had been able to have some semblance of happiness out in this harsh environment, raised by this uncompromising man? Or had the years been filled with torture and abuse, the way Sadie feared?

And now she'd gone. Sadie knew the trail would be icy cold, but she was FBI and she could find her. Jessica Price had been presumed drowned. But Belinda Price had been living here, alive and well, and perhaps, somehow, this brutal, murderous man had found the redemption with her that he'd craved.

Sadie looked down at the picture. Her own eyes, her own sister. She was alive and well. She had embarked on her adult life. And now, Sadie knew where. All she had to do was find her.

EPILOGUE

"I'd better go." Sadie checked the time, listening to the bustle of the airport around her, the comings and goings of people, the whirring of travel bag wheels and the clatter of trolleys.

"You go. You find her."

Cooper stood up from the kiosk where they'd been having a last coffee together. He walked with her the short distance to airport security.

In half an hour, she would be boarding the flight to San Francisco.

Who could tell what the next couple of days would bring?

She felt nervous but excited, as if a circle was being completed at last - a circle that had spent a lifetime so far playing out. And now, it was time to join it, to heal, to seek the friend and companion, the sister she thought she'd lost forever. Who had kept her side of the deal, kept her secrets, because she'd loved Sadie.

Assuming she could find Jessica at all. There was always the chance that she would have disappeared, moved on, gone elsewhere, even traveled overseas. She might be untraceable, but Sadie knew she had to try. She was hopeful. She'd looked up her new name, used the might of the FBI databases to help her, and found a recent recorded address for Belinda Price in the Marina District. There was no phone number, so she planned to arrive there in person and see what played out.

"Travel well. I'll take care of everything here. Make sure everyone keeps in line, and stays safe," Cooper joked.

"I'll be back soon. Work starts on Monday. And then I'll be having the meeting with Golightly, and signing the documents," Sadie said. "I've already accepted his offer. I told him my future is here. I'm going to be taking up the position of senior agent."

She saw in Cooper's eyes exactly what that meant to him.

They hugged and kissed. For a moment, Sadie allowed herself to relax in his arms, feeling his strength, knowing this was where she belonged.

"I'll stay in touch. And I'll be home before you know it," she said.

She'd called it home, she realized, surprised. And to her, right now, it was. This had become her home, and it was where she would return. She was looking forward to coming home. But for now, she had an important mission to complete.

Wheeling her bag, Sadie walked away, taking the first step on a new journey, one she'd never dreamed she would be making.

"Jessica," she whispered. "Please be there. Please. I can't wait to see you again."

TOO LATE
(A Morgan Stark FBI Suspense Thriller—Book 1)

Morgan Stark, a brilliant doctor, is stunned when his hospital's resident is found murdered, clearly the work of a serial killer. The FBI needs Morgan, with his medical expertise, to decipher the subtle medical clues that will lead to the killer—but can he crack the code before it's too late?

"A brilliant book. I couldn't put it down and I never guessed who the murderer was!"
—Reader review for Only Murder

TOO LATE is the debut novel in a new series by #1 bestselling and critically acclaimed mystery and suspense author Rylie Dark.

Morgan Stark is a renowned surgeon, acclaimed by his colleagues for his brilliance as a diagnostician. But when his close friend and protégé resident is murdered, Morgan feels compelled to help the FBI decipher the trail of medical clues and bring the killer to justice.

FBI Special Agent Danielle Hernandez, 28, a rising star in the BAU, equally esteemed by her colleagues for her brilliance and determination, is not used to turning to a doctor for help in solving crimes. This unlikely partnership, though, may just surprise them both.

Yet as brilliant as this team is, they are up against a diabolical mastermind who will stop at nothing to outwit them.

And going too deep into his mind may just undo them both.

A cat-and-mouse thriller with harrowing twists and turns and filled with heart-pounding suspense, the MORGAN STARK mystery series offers a fresh twist on the genre as it introduces two brilliant protagonists who will make you fall in love and keep you turning pages late into the night.

Rylie Dark

Bestselling author Rylie Dark is author of the SADIE PRICE FBI SUSPENSE THRILLER series, comprising six books (and counting); the MIA NORTH FBI SUSPENSE THRILLER series, comprising six books (and counting); the CARLY SEE FBI SUSPENSE THRILLER, comprising six books (and counting); and the MORGAN STARK FBI SUSPENSE THRILLER, comprising three books (and counting).

An avid reader and lifelong fan of the mystery and thriller genres, Rylie loves to hear from you, so please feel free to visit www.ryliedark.com to learn more and stay in touch.

BOOKS BY RYLIE DARK

SADIE PRICE FBI SUSPENSE THRILLER
ONLY MURDER (Book #1)
ONLY RAGE (Book #2)
ONLY HIS (Book #3)
ONLY ONCE (Book #4)
ONLY SPITE (Book #5)
ONLY MADNESS (Book #6)

MIA NORTH FBI SUSPENSE THRILLER
SEE HER RUN (Book #1)
SEE HER HIDE (Book #2)
SEE HER SCREAM (Book #3)
SEE HER VANISH (Book #4)
SEE HER GONE (Book #5)
SEE HER DEAD (Book #6)

CARLY SEE FBI SUSPENSE THRILLER
NO WAY OUT (Book #1)
NO WAY BACK (Book #2)
NO WAY HOME (Book #3)
NO WAY LEFT (Book #4)
NO WAY UP (Book #5)
NO WAY TO DIE (Book #6)

MORGAN STARK FBI SUSPENSE THRILLER
TOO LATE (Book #1)
TOO CLOSE (Book #2)
TOO FAR GONE (Book #3)

Made in the USA
Columbia, SC
29 December 2022